RIPL.   ..AYES

A Man

A Gay Mystery

First edition

This book was professionally typeset on Reedsy.
Find out more at reedsy.com

Contents

Foreword

Wales...

The Daniel Owen books are set in north Wales. The towns and landscapes are typical of places in Wales, but these are novels, not guidebooks. You can visit stunning forests, mountains, beaches, towns and villages that may remind you of the ones in these books and you will find that they are almost crime-free and full of friendly people, independent shops and cafes serving good food. But none of the places in these books exist, except in my imagination.

The Welsh language is spoken all over the country. In some places you will hear more Welsh than English, in others, English is the default. Legally the two languages have equal status, signs and official documents are in both, and every Welsh schoolchild either has Welsh lessons or is taught entirely through the medium of Welsh. The Welsh Government encourages adults to learn. I'm a Welsh learner, dividing my time between one area where Welsh is the default, and one where it is English. All these books have a few words in Welsh which I try to make clear in the context. I double check all the Welsh I use, but any mistakes are mine and I apologise for them.

Place Names

Melin Tywyll (phonetically something like Mellin Too-uth) is an imaginary town in north Wales. The name means Dark Mill, a hint at its past. It is set in the Black River Valley (Cwm Afon Ddu, phonetically Koom Avon Thee), also entirely imaginary. Gelli (Gethli) is a hamlet on the outskirts. The letters 'C' and 'G' are always hard in Welsh.

Heddlu Clwyd (Hethlee Kloo-ud) is an imaginary north Wales police force. Clwyd is the traditional name for the area of north Wales covered by the modern counties of Wrexham, Conwy, Denbighshire and Flintshire.

Glamorgan Police (Heddlu Morgannwg, Hethlee Morgann-ug) is an imaginary south Wales police force. Glamorgan is the area of Wales covering the south coast from Cardiff to the Gower, and the Valleys to the north.

Chapter 1

* * *

The two little girls looked as if they were sleeping peacefully. He covered them gently, half-wishing it were true.

Daniel Owen had persuaded his boyfriend Mal out of bed, into shorts and trainers, out of the door, all before 6 am. Daniel wanted Mal to see the glories of the early summer woods, to hear the birds going mad, to smell the earth and feel the breeze on his bare skin. They'd had a hard winter, Mal recovering from being shot, and both of them trying to forget the terror of that night in the Burns and Wood building. Daniel believed in the healing power of trees, and Mal didn't put up much of a fight — he had a plan for the shower when they got back.

They warmed up along level tracks though the woods from the house, increasing the pace easily as they descended a tarmac lane between high hedges, dense and busy with birds. Where the road straightened, they saw hills stretching into the distance, hazy in the early sunlight. Mal reached for Daniel's hand. Daniel thought that he hadn't run hand-in-hand with anyone since infant school.

"This is great. We should do this more often," Mal said, and smiled, because Daniel had been trying for weeks to get him to swap the air-conditioned gym for a run outside.

"Let's see how you feel when we're going up the other side." Daniel said.

Daniel liked the middle section of the run best. The long level sweep from the bottom of the hill, through the hamlet of Gelli and almost into the outskirts of the town of Melin Tywyll, over a packhorse bridge onto 'their' side of the river, and on until the climb back to Bryn Carreg and home. By that point, he would have found his rhythm, counting in his head, his mind empty of everything except maintaining his pace, and saving enough energy to get up the hill ahead. It kept him sane, or as much as anything could after their last case. On a day like this, with Mal to chat to, he could stay in the moment and the past faded away.

As they ran towards Gelli, and its few houses, Daniel saw something in the road ahead. Mal saw it too. A small child, wearing not much more than a nappy and wellies, toddling towards them with some determination.

"He shouldn't be out on his own," Mal said, and they slowed to a walk as they grew closer.

"Hi!" said Daniel, dropping into a crouch, "What are you doing little fella? Where's your Mam?"

Assigning the male gender seemed reasonable. The child had a T-shirt with dinosaurs, and the wellies were a blue camouflage pattern.

The child looked up at them with big dark blue eyes.

"Dada," he said, and started to cry.

* * *

The child was too young to say which one was his house, or to tell them his name. Daniel took his hand and led him to the side of the road, sitting on the verge, to get down to his level. Mal went to knock on the nearest door, a house that fronted onto the road, hoping for a resident who wouldn't be freaked out by a sweaty, bare-chested man in shorts at 6.30 in the morning. He was unlucky. No one answered. Next door was set further back, and was a bigger house. A well-trodden path led up the side to what he assumed was the kitchen door, and the one most obviously used. The door swung open as he knocked on it. One look was enough; though in truth, he knew before he looked. As the door opened, the smell of blood came at him in a wave, mixed with other, even less pleasant smells. He didn't want to go in, but there wasn't a choice. If someone was alive, it was his job to find them.

He didn't need medical training to tell that the two people in the kitchen were dead. Next to the door, a body lay with its head blown off, a sawn-off shotgun on the floor beside it, one hand still holding the trigger. On the other side of the room another figure had slumped against the wall, its body a mass of blood and intestines where the shot had ripped it apart in the middle. Blood was thick everywhere, brains and bits of bone splattered the floor and walls. The buzzing of flies filled the air. His goal was the door on the other side of the room, and he made it by holding his breath and placing each foot with all the care he could muster.

The hallway beyond the kitchen was carpeted, and his feet were quiet, quiet enough that he could hear the sound of flies ahead of him, as well as at his back. He felt sick. He found the source of the flies behind the door — the remains of a yellow Labrador retriever. The rest of the room was clear, just a normal room, with sofas and a TV. The curtains were closed and the lights on.

There was also a dining room, though the table was covered with oilcloth and children's paints, crayons and modelling clay. A computer desk was pushed up against the wall by the door, and an electronic keyboard by the window. Back in the hall, the cupboard under the stairs held nothing more sinister than the vacuum cleaner and a mop bucket.

The upstairs had a generous landing leading to four bedrooms and a bathroom. All the doors were open, although again, some of the curtains were drawn. The first room must have been a guest room, with a double bed, neatly made, but holding a slew of winter coats, and what looked like children's clothes, ironed and folded. The curtains were open. The next room had a king-sized bed, with the duvet thrown back, as if someone had got up in a hurry, and the room next to it had a baby's cot, along with an ironing board and a sewing machine. The other door had two plaques, *Seren* and *Stella*. He didn't want to go in. The room had two single beds; one on each side of a big window. The curtains were pink, and closed. Each bed had a pretty pink duvet cover, and on each bed a girl's head lay on a pink covered pillow, dark hair spilling over her face, her body neatly tucked in. Both girls were surrounded by stuffed animals, and between the beds a tumble of books and toys. There was no sound of breathing, and neither girl reacted to the door opening. He moved towards the nearest bed, and looked at the pale face, eyes closed, long lashes resting on her cheeks. He reached over, but she was as cold as ice.

* * *

Mal let himself out of the front door, unwilling to risk the dreadful kitchen again, and found Daniel still holding the little boy. Daniel saw Mal's face, closed and tight, with tears on his cheeks, and he knew what was in the house.

"Phone," Mal said, and Daniel handed it over. Mal moved back towards the house, and Daniel caught snippets.

"Fatalities... shotgun ... pathologist ... small child ... social worker ... and a couple of tracksuits for the DI and myself, we were out running."

Daniel raised his eyebrows as Mal returned. Mal shook his head, indicating the child. The little boy was trying to pull away from Daniel, and crying "Dada, Dada." Daniel stood and scooped him up, saying "Shall we go and find your Dada? Hey *Cariad*? Let's have a look this way." They walked away from the house, Daniel pointing out birds, and flowers, speaking in both Welsh and English, until the child settled into Daniel's arms and started throwing out single words in response to Daniel's questions. The baby felt warm and heavy in Daniel's embrace, an antidote to horror.

My life should have more babies and fewer bodies.

The door to the first house opened.

"What's going on?" demanded an elderly man in a stained dressing gown, one hearing aid dangling half-in and half-out of his ear. "I'll ring the police." The man produced a mobile phone and held it out in front of him, as if possession alone would protect him.

"I know we don't look like it, sir, but we are the police." Mal was acutely aware of his nipple ring and Daniel's tattoos. "My name is DCI Maldwyn Kent, and the man with the baby is DI Daniel Owen. There has been a serious incident at your neighbours' house. Our colleagues are on their way." The man didn't look convinced.

"Ring Melin Tywyll police, sir, they will confirm our identities." But it wasn't necessary, because the first patrol car arrived, without sirens, but blue lights flashing. A uniformed constable got out and said, "Sir," although the look of amusement wasn't far below the surface.

"I was out for a run, Jones," said Mal, resisting the temptation to suggest PC Jones, and his large belly would benefit from doing the same. "I need you to keep a list of everyone who goes up the path to that house, and there are going to be a lot of them, believe me. Get yourself

5

a clipboard, and do it now."

The man in the dressing gown looked as if his eyes would burst from his head; *out on stalks like chapel hat pegs*, as his mother would have said.

"One of my officers will be round shortly to ask you for a statement, sir," said Mal, "Why don't you go back inside and get dressed?"

* * *

The heart wants what the heart wants, thought Hector. At the moment his heart wanted the tall thin woman lying next to him in bed. Sasha's daughter Arwen was asleep in the bedroom next door, and in the morning they'd promised her an outing to the seaside, but for now it was just them. He wrapped his arms around Sasha and breathed in her scent. She sighed and snuggled closer, her body making lewd suggestions.

There was a cry of "*Mama*" from next door.

"I'll settle her down, and be right back," said Sasha, with an exaggerated wink. She got out of the bed, wrapping herself in the dressing gown hanging behind the door, and he heard her say, "Mama's coming." He and Sasha had planned this week for ages, and nothing was going to spoil it. He could hear singing from next door and smiled. Sasha had a terrible voice, and could never remember more than a few words of any song. She made no distinction between lullabies and the last thing she heard on the radio. But after a moment, the singing died away and Sasha was back.

"Is she OK?" Hector asked.

"Woke up in a strange place, and she'd thrown Big Bear out of the bed," Sasha said, "She'll probably do it again, so if you want to get your leg over, we'd better be quick."

"I'm game," he said.

Arwen was a smaller version of her mother, Hector thought. Already growing tall and eating as much as someone twice her age, with no obvious effect on her shape. There had never been any talk of a father, but whoever he was, he hadn't contributed much in the way of genes. He also wasn't contributing any money — Sasha worked as a night cleaner, and lived in a small rented house in a cheap area of the south Wales Valleys. Hector was a pathologist, and spent his days with the dead. It was all he'd wanted to do since he started medical school, and discovered the delights of secrets revealed beneath the skin. Fellow students had wanted to become surgeons, or oncologists, neurologists — almost everything with living patients seemed more desirable than pathology. But Sasha understood. She was about to become a student of biomedical science, and that's what they talked about, that and the little girl who was beginning to call him Uncle Hector, and who was winding her tiny fingers around his heart.

Chapter 2

He looked down at the little bodies and felt the love for them overflow. *No more suffering, no more betrayal.*

Hector's work phone rang as he and Sasha were making breakfast. Arwen was watching cartoons on Hector's computer.

"I don't let her stare at screens all day," Sasha said.

"I know," Hector replied.

"It's what working class mothers are always accused of. Plonking their kids in front of the telly and feeding them junk."

"You don't do that."

"Lots of middle class parents do it. They just give their kids *organic* junk. And make them look at wildlife videos, because they don't have the Disney channel."

Hector didn't have a TV at all.

"And middle class parents who buy second hand clothes are saving the planet. Working class mothers are being cheap. I'd rather have Arwen in good quality second hand stuff than new from Primark. Or a catalogue. Of course, I'm a single parent so nothing I do is going to be right anyway."

Hector wondered what had brought on this un-Sasha-like bout of insecurity. He asked her.

"Nothing," she said.

Hector raised his eyebrows.

"OK. Your neighbour, that old woman. I said hello and she looked away like I was dirt. We were just getting out of the car, and Arwen was whinging, and she'd got chocolate all over her face. It's a long drive, and she'd had one biscuit, that's all."

"Sasha, listen, I think you're a great parent. My parents sent me away to school when I was seven, that's a year older than Arwen is now. If I had a TV, I would get the Disney channel just for Arwen. And I'd watch it with her, and make wholemeal sugarless popcorn."

"No way. She's going to be watching autopsy videos with her Mam."

"And taking holidays to the Body Farm."

"Looking forward to explaining that at parent's evenings."

Hector thought that she would, and that he might like to be there too.

Arwen was oblivious until the phone rang. Then she looked up and called out, "Uncle Hector, phone."

Hector saw who was calling and pulled a face. He listened and answered with grunts, and finally asked for directions.

"I've got to go, and it'll be a few hours," he said, "I'm so sorry." This is it, he thought, this is where it all starts to go wrong. But Sasha just pulled a face, said "*poor you*", and then said that they could go to the seaside when he got back, as long as he didn't mind them hanging about in his house without him. From what he'd just heard from Mal, the seaside with Sasha and Arwen would be a necessary antidote. He dealt with death in all its forms, but dead children were the hardest.

"The ice-cream will be on me," he said. He opened a drawer in the kitchen table and rooted around amongst the receipts and mismatched cutlery, producing a key on a ring. "House key," he said, "in case you want to go out."

"Shall I put some of this bacon into a sandwich?" Sasha asked, and he shook his head.

9

"I don't think I'm going to want to eat," he said.

She put her arms round him. "You're a nice man, Dr Lord," she said, and he thought that for the first time ever, he would rather stay at home than go to work.

* * *

Calling Gelli a hamlet was overstating the case. It was six houses and a derelict barn. Five of the houses formed a terrace with only a couple of steps stopping their front doors from opening directly onto the road. The other house stood further back, between the terrace and the derelict barn. It was this house, *Ty Gelli* according to the carved slate sign, where PC Jones was recording the procession of Crime Scene Investigators in and out.

The other houses were numbered, but there appeared to be no street name. If there was a street name, Mal thought, the residents and postman would know it, and for everyone else, the road would be "the road by Gelli." It was a pretty spot in the early morning sunshine. Mal checked the compass on his phone — unlike a lot of places deep within a valley, Gelli faced south, so wouldn't spend half the year in darkness. Not at the front anyway.

Behind the houses, the hillside rose steeply, covered in trees, leaving enough room for a yard behind each of the terraced houses. *Ty Gelli* had a garden around three sides. The back had been quarried out, the stone probably used to build the houses, and between the house and the derelict barn there was a polytunnel, a fruit cage, and half a dozen raised beds. Mal heard the murmuring of chickens, still in their coop, although the coop itself was out of sight. He thought that whoever lived there had ideas of the good life, and judging from the healthy state of the plants in the raised beds, they were succeeding.

On the opposite side of the road to the houses, the land was flat, with gravelled parking spaces leading to gardens, with more evidence of fruit and vegetable growing, and beyond the gardens, to well-fenced fields with sheep. The river was out of sight, just a stream here, if he remembered rightly, draining into the Afon Ddu by the packhorse bridge. This was a dead-end valley, running roughly east-west, hard to get to by car.

The terraced houses looked well maintained. His colleagues had knocked, and he'd seen worried faces above a mixture of nightwear and what looked like the first clothes that came to hand. The residents were a mix of men and women. With the exception of the old man who'd spoken to him already, everyone seemed young, one woman had a baby in her arms, and another appeared with a toddler on her hip. The men he saw all had big beards and one had long hair to match. Mal told himself not to reach any conclusions based on three beardy men and a couple of women in patchwork skirts. Not when he was dressed in shorts and not much else. On the other hand, he lived with Daniel Owen, and he recognised the signs of the alternative life: the stacks of wood, the handbuilt sheds, and the old tyres painted bright colours and stacked up as planters for potatoes. He also noticed that once they'd had a look at what was going on, the young people all disappeared together into number two and the door closed behind them.

* * *

Daniel held the little boy close. He was soft and warm against Daniel's

11

bare chest, though his runny nose and tears had left Daniel's skin wet. Daniel chattered on in Welsh, hoping that he'd made the right choice of language, but the little one was distressed again. He was probably hungry, Daniel thought, quite apart from needing his parents. The desire he had to make things right for the child shocked Daniel. He put the thought aside for later, and tried everything he could think of to calm the baby down,

From what he had overheard Mal say on the phone, Daniel had a good idea of what had happened in the house. *Family annihilation* was the term they used, when someone, almost always a husband and father, killed everyone close to them. Except, in this case, one child.

Daniel had heard Mal ask for a social worker, and he was sure that there would be a foster carer lined up soon. But he didn't think that the little boy could wait much longer for something to eat. He hoped the ambulance would arrive soon. One of the front doors opened, and a man with a long beard and longer hair stepped out. He wore battered jeans and an equally battered T-shirt, but no shoes.

"Is that Dafydd?" the man asked, looking at the child, seeming unperturbed by Daniel's appearance.

"I don't know his name," he said, "we found him in the road."

"It looks like Dafydd. What's happened? Are the family OK?"

As the road was now packed with police cars, Daniel thought the guy could probably answer his own question.

"I can't tell you anything, sir, I'm sorry. But do you know how old this one is?"

A woman appeared in the doorway, the woman he'd seen before with a baby.

"Do you want me to take him?" she asked Daniel.

Daniel shook his head. "But can you tell me anything about him?"

The woman nodded, "Sure. Shift, Cai, let me out." She fixed her eyes on Daniel, "I'm Mel."

Daniel stepped back as Mel came out of the house, and stroked the little boy's head. It seemed to calm him. The bearded man said, "So, who are you mate? How come you've got Dafydd and not one of them?" He gestured at the police cars and their occupants.

Daniel snuggled the toddler closer. "I am one of them," he said, "Detective Inspector Owen. I don't usually dress like this for work."

"Cai. Love the ink, man,"

This had to be the weirdest day of his police career, ever, Daniel thought, as the child struggled in his arms and started crying.

"Maybe the little 'un needs a nappy change," Cai said. And Daniel thought, *no he doesn't. And that's a bit strange too.*

"He's fine," said Daniel, "just hungry I think."

"They're good people," Cai said, looking up the road, "the Edwardses. Dafydd's folks. John and Hayley. Two little girls as well as this one. Seren and Stella. Nice to have lots of kids."

"He's about 12 months," Mel said, "unexpected treat I think, the girls are older. Are they OK?"

"I'm sorry, I can't tell you anything at the moment." Daniel said again, and saw the ambulance arrive. "Excuse me," he said.

* * *

Daniel didn't recognise the paramedics, but they knew who he was. They ignored his appearance and listened to what he had to say.

"We found him in the road, walking towards us. Dafydd Edwards. One of the neighbours thinks he's about a year old, I think he's hungry, but his nappy is dry."

The paramedic asked if Daniel was coming with them. "Give me a minute," he said, handing the little boy to one of the paramedics who began, very gently, to check him over.

Daniel jogged over to Mal, who had found a black T-shirt with Police stencilled across the back.

"Shall I go with the baby? Or do you need me here?"

"Go," said Mal, "no one can do anything here. It's too late."

"They're all dead then. The little girls too?"

Mal nodded. "Ring me when you know something about the baby. And get a T-shirt from PC Morgan."

"Mal, when did they die?"

"Last night at a guess, I touched the girls and they were icy, and the curtains were closed. But we can't be sure until Hector's seen them."

"So where has Dafydd been since then?" Daniel asked, "because he's hungry, and fed up, but he's not hysterical or injured, and his nappy is clean."

"Go," said Mal again. "Trust me on this, we are going to find out what happened here."

"You know this was Hector's week with Sasha." Daniel said.

"Not any more," said Mal.

PC Morgan tapped Daniel on the shoulder. "Track suit, sir?" He held out a navy blue police issue track suit. "It's a bit big, but it's the best we could do."

Daniel took the garments and looked down at himself. His shorts were his lightweight racing shorts, and a long way from being suitable for respectable company. He smiled at PC Morgan.

"Thanks, mate, better than being arrested for public indecency."

He put the track suit jacket on and PC Morgan couldn't help a grin. "It was PC Jones's, sir." The two of them looked over at PC Jones, sweltering, even in his short-sleeved shirt, buttons straining to cover his belly.

"He's fitter than he looks. Just big."

The trousers were even more ridiculous. "Well no one will see my arse with these on," Daniel said, grateful for the drawstring fastening.

In the ambulance, the paramedic had Dafydd wrapped in a blanket, wellies and all. "He's a bit dehydrated, but apart from that he seems OK," she said. "But we'll get him to hospital, and they can have a proper look and get some fluids in. There's a social worker meeting us there. Poor little kid. I'm guessing his parents didn't make it. Do you want to hold him?"

Daniel did, and was rewarded with a faint smile. His heart turned over.

"We don't know who he is for certain," Daniel said, "so I can't tell you, sorry." He was getting tired of saying it. It felt wrong not to be able to share with a fellow professional, but the consequences of a mistaken identity, and worse, a mistaken identity leaked to the press, didn't bear thinking about. The paramedic withdrew, and didn't speak again until they arrived at the hospital.

Daniel was pleased to see his friend Veronica was waiting for them. "Duty social worker," she said, I'm assuming this little one is my responsibility?"

"Until we find his relatives," Daniel said.

"And maybe afterwards," she replied.

* * *

The young man looked as if he was willing to wait. Bethan had tried to tell him that there had been a major incident, and that DCI Kent was not available, nor likely to be for a long time.

"This afternoon? Will he be back this afternoon? I could go and have a walk round and come back."

Bethan sighed. She had two sons at university and this boy looked to be the same sort of age, only much cleaner and tidier than her own two. She loved them, but her efforts to persuade them to keep on top of laundry fell on stony ground. This young man didn't need her lessons. His chinos and linen shirt had been pressed by someone who knew what they were doing, and he had the shirt sleeves rolled up to exactly the same point on each arm. His brown hair had been recently trimmed, and whatever product he'd used was keeping it in place. Unlike her own sons, the young man smelled of something expensive — no Lynx for this one. He had a small leather backpack resting by his feet.

"I don't know," she said, "I am literally the only detective in the building, and I have a thousand things to do. I suggest you leave him a note."

The young man nodded and said that would be fine, "if you're sure that he'll get it."

"You write it, I'll personally put it on his desk." She asked the civilian at the front desk for a pen and paper, and the young man took it and quickly wrote a mobile phone number and a name: *Jamie Maddocks.* He folded it in half and handed it to Bethan with a shy smile. The name meant nothing to her, but she took the note and promised that it would be on the DCI's desk as soon as she could get back up the stairs.

Chapter 3

The sharks had circled them for years. One mistake, after years and years of doing what was expected — and they all lived in fear.

The second time Mal went into *Ty Gelli* he was suitably dressed in a paper suit, bootees and gloves. He'd probably left traces of himself from his first visit, but he wasn't going to add any more. This time he wasn't alone, but that didn't make the scene in the kitchen any less shocking.

The figure by the door was almost headless, the neck ending in a mash of blood, bone and grey matter. The body was dressed in jeans and a sweatshirt, with the feet in trainers. The shape and size of the figure suggested that it was male. On the other side of the kitchen, the second figure had been female. She had long brown hair, and had been wearing a dressing gown, now saturated with her blood. Her feet were bare and Mal saw that she had painted her toenails in a glittery pink. The wall behind her body was smeared with blood where she had been blown into it and then slid down.

"Bastard killed his family, then himself," said Paul Jarvis, the senior CSI.

"We don't know that yet," said Mal, "we don't know anything yet, so don't behave as if we do."

Jarvis looked over his face mask as if he had seen it all before, and Mal was a rookie.

"Do you even know whether this man fired the gun he's touching?" asked Mal, and Jarvis flushed, whether from anger or embarrassment, Mal couldn't tell. But the answer was a clear, if unspoken, *No.*

"Anyone could have fired that weapon," Mal said.

"Sure, anyone *could have*," said Jarvis, "but how likely is it?"

"That," said Mal, in a voice that would have frozen steam, "is what Clwyd Police is paying you to find out. If we wanted guesswork we could do it ourselves." One of the other investigators pulled Jarvis away before he said anything irreparable. Mal made a mental note to double check everything Jarvis signed off. He heard a familiar voice outside, and picked his way back to the door, only stepping on the marked footsteps they were allowed to use.

Hector was already in his paper suit. They touched each other briefly on the arm, and Mal said, "This is the worst I've seen in a long time. The adults are bad enough, but the two little girls ... Forensics have already started, but no one has touched the bodies, just taken photographs."

Hector nodded and said "Can you come round with me? So I can show you anything, *in situ,* so to speak?"

"As long as you don't mind interruptions. We're trying to confirm identity and get witness statements. Where do you want to start?"

Hector looked through the kitchen door at the two smashed bodies. "Were the children shot?"

Mal shook his head. "No. I couldn't see any obvious cause of death." "Then let's start with them."

Mal led Hector round to the front door, now open, and into the hall. "Upstairs," he said.

At the top of the stairs, Mal paused. "Deep breath time," he said to Hector.

They moved towards the girls' bedroom, and the bodies of the

18

children.

The bedroom was gloomy, but Mal took in more details this time. He could see that the walls were painted a pale blue, with some kind of flowers, and what looked like fairies, painted on top. The beds were wood, painted white. Only a little light seeped round the pink curtains, suggesting a blind to keep the room dark. Most of the light came from the open door behind him. Hector was standing by the bed to the left of the window. The white headboard had more flowers and fairies and woven amongst the waving fronds was the word *Stella*.

She was lying on her back, arms in front of her, dark hair framing her face, in pyjamas covered in tiny unicorns, eyes closed. Freckles stood out against her pale skin.

Hector crouched down beside her, feeling the skin of her neck. His heart jumped, once, painfully, into his throat. This child was more rounded and darker than Arwen, but she was surely the same age. He had a sudden urge to pull his phone out from under the paper suit, and ring Sasha, just to check that the two of them were OK. He swallowed. He felt Mal's hand on his arm.

"Me too," Mal said, "she's the same sort of age as Daniel's niece."

"Get your notebook out, Detective Chief Inspector, because we are going to nail whoever did this."

Hector took the temperature of the girl's body, tried to move the stiffened limbs, and finally opened the eyes, peering down closely. He took the temperature of the room. He moved the bedclothes aside and the little girl's pyjamas. Then he stood up.

"I think this is where she was killed." Hector pointed to a cushion on the floor. "That, or something like it, is the murder weapon. She was smothered."

"Can you tell when they died?"

"Educated guess ... I'd say last night, but you could work that out for yourself. The curtains are closed, little girl wearing pyjamas, rigor

19

mortis very evident. It's warm, so the body temperature isn't very helpful."

"Tell me the rest."

"So, the signs of asphyxiation are all there, mostly burst blood vessels in the eyes. And I know she was killed here, because the blood has pooled around the back and buttocks, suggesting that she died on her back. But because it's so warm, I can't say anything for sure. As for why? That's your job."

"Was the other girl killed the same way?" Mal asked. They looked over to the other bed. This time the name picked out between the flowers was *Seren*. Again, the girl lay on her back, hair around her face, pale skin almost translucent in the half light. This girl was older, maybe nine or ten.

For the second time that morning, Mal felt the tears running down his face, and all he could do was wipe them away with the sleeve of his paper suit.

The little girl was dressed in the same unicorn patterned pyjamas as her sister.

"Were they asleep?" Mal asked.

"I can't tell," said Hector, kneeling by the body, and touching her gently. Mal had to look away.

"I can tell you that she was almost certainly smothered, and that the two girls died at roughly the same time. If the same pillow was used, it should have DNA from both of them, and they should both have fibres from the cover in their noses and lungs."

They had to leave the bodies where they were until the photographers and crime scenes officers had finished. Mal hated the thought of them lying alone and unattended, cast away like two dolls. He wanted to stay with them, until when, he didn't know. Leaving seemed like yet another betrayal of the innocent. But it was time to go into the kitchen and deal with the mess in there.

Walkways were marked out in the kitchen, stickers and flags showing where pieces of evidence had been found. Hector approached the woman first.

"No doubt about the cause of this death?" Mal asked.

"No doubt that she was alive when she was shot," Hector replied, "so it's a reasonable assumption. But that's all it can be for now." Moving the body was going to be difficult — the gunshot had almost cut the woman in half. The dead woman was in her nightclothes — thin pyjamas, and a lightweight cotton dressing gown. Her feet were bare, toenails painted. Her hair was the same dark brown as the two girls, and worn loose. But everything on her body was soaked in her blood, as was the wall behind her and the floor onto which she'd fallen.

The obvious reading of the scene was that she'd come into the room and been shot by the man with the gun. And then the man had turned the gun on himself. But if this was a man killing his wife and family, why was the boy spared?

* * *

"What do we know about him?" Veronica asked, as they watched the doctor and nurses check the little boy for any injuries. They took his vital signs, and organised a bottle of formula, and a nappy change. The ward was bright and cheerful with cots rather than beds, pictures and mobiles around the walls and several boxes of toys in odd corners. Not all the cots were occupied, but those that were had at least one visitor each, talking quietly to their child, or playing with them. The children themselves, from what Daniel could see, all looked ill. Except little Dafydd, who looked like any other toddler. A bit nervous to be amongst strangers, but interested, his eyes fastening on one of the toy boxes.

"Only what I already told you," said Daniel. We were out for a run, and there he was, toddling towards us in wellies, a T-shirt and his nappy. Mal started knocking on doors, and found the bodies of two adults and two children."

"And you think that's his family?"

"I don't think anything yet," said Daniel, "Mal says that he thinks the people in the house died last night. If that's true, then this little one must have been somewhere else. He wasn't nearly hungry or dirty enough to have been on his own since last night. Not that I'm an expert, but I remember my nephew and niece."

Veronica was scribbling notes, most of which, Daniel saw, involved question marks.

"You say the neighbours said he was from the house with the bodies? And said he was called Dafydd?"

Daniel nodded. "We'll start looking for relatives as soon as we're done here."

Daniel looked over to the bed where little Dafydd was sitting in the arms of a young nurse, guzzling greedily at his bottle. The doctor — another young woman — came across to them.

"He's fine," she said with a smile. "Well cared for, about eighteen months old. He has a few words, not many, and he seems happy enough now he's getting something to eat. We'll give him some solids in a bit." Her words were directed towards Veronica. Veronica put her briefcase on a chair and opened it, producing a slim file.

"He's in the care of Clwyd Social Services, until further notice," she said, and handed a copy of a document to the doctor, who clipped it onto the notes at the end of the bed. "So any clinical decisions, or any other decisions, need to be referred to us, and we'll liaise with the police about tracking down his relatives, if he has any." Veronica said that they would find a foster carer as quickly as they could, but for now, it looked like Dafydd would be staying where he was.

The doctor looked out of the corner of her eye at Daniel, and he remembered that he was dressed in PC Jones's oversized track suit. He explained who he was, and said Veronica would vouch for him.

"We took one phone between us, and I've left it with my partner. No warrant card, sorry."

Veronica smiled. "He's usually rather smart," she said, "and he really is a Detective Inspector."

"Trust me," Daniel looked at the two women, "this outfit would not be my first choice, but it's much better than the alternative."

At that moment, the little boy finished his bottle. He looked up and saw Daniel, and his face broke into a huge, heartbreaking grin.

"Hi," said Daniel, smiling back.

"Hi," said the child, clear as a bell, "Man."

With the little boy in safe hands, Daniel felt that it would be OK to nip home for proper clothes for him and Mal. Mal would be at the scene at least until the bodies were removed, and neither of them had eaten more than a banana since the early morning. He made a flask of coffee, a box of sandwiches, shoved chocolate on top, showered and dressed as fast as he could, then picked up clothes for Mal, and set off, the very long way round by road, back to Gelli.

* * *

Screens had been set up around the doorway and between the house and the road. Daniel knew what the screens meant, and his hands shook. The image of DI Andy Carter dying in the Burns and Wood building last winter filled his eyes. A gangster called Wade Addison had killed Carter in cold blood, just to make the point that he could. Then he shot Mal, and Daniel had been too frightened to stop him. Carter had been a bent cop. Two of the dead in *Ty Gelli* were children, but they were still killed

Chapter 4

H e had run. He had hidden. *Someone always betrayed him to the sharks. This time he would keep them all safe.*

Mal knew that hovering around the crime scene wasn't going to make the investigators move any faster. He asked Paul Jarvis to prioritise anything to give them information about possible relatives for Dafydd. Jarvis was still bristling after Mal's earlier harsh words, but he called Mal back inside after the children's bodies had been removed. Mal suited up again.

"We've found a strong box. Not locked, somewhere for important documents, keep them safe in a fire."

The box was opened on the dining table, documents spread out around it.

"We'll bag everything up," said Jarvis, "but I thought that you'd want a quick look first."

Mal did. There were four passports, four birth certificates, a marriage certificate, wills, property deeds, and other financial papers. He opened the passports. The first photograph showed a man with short dark hair and brown eyes, who might have been attractive in anything other than a passport picture. His birth certificate showed him to have been forty-one when he died.

"John Edwards," said Mal, "do we know what he did for a living?"

Jarvis shook his head, but pulled a certificate from the pile.

"He has a first class degree in Business Studies from the Open University, and the marriage certificate gives his profession as 'sport' and no other details," Jarvis said, "Though that doesn't mean much. We'll keep looking."

Mal moved on to the woman's passport. Another dark haired, brown-eyed face looked out, and Mal thought how odd it was that some couples looked like each other. These two could almost be brother and sister. Mrs Edwards, Hayley, was the same age as her husband. The marriage certificate showed them to have been married for twelve years. Mal copied the names of the couple's fathers from the marriage certificate — John Edwards, and John Patterson.

"We do know what Mrs Edwards did," said Jarvis, "or rather we know what she was qualified to do." He gave Mal a small bundle of nursing qualifications, mostly for Hayley Patterson, one or two more recent ones for Hayley Edwards.

The children's birth certificates showed Seren to have been the eldest at ten, and her sister Stella to have been three years younger.

"Those poor girls," said Mal, feeling ready to weep again, as he looked at the passports.

"I know." Jarvis said, and Mal thought this case was going to have an impact on a lot of people. Jarvis didn't sound cocky any more, he sounded as sad as Mal.

"Nothing for the little boy?" Mal asked, even though he could see that there wasn't.

"Nothing," Jarvis confirmed.

"But there's a nursery upstairs."

"I'm not sure it was in use," said Jarvis, "and I'm sure you've seen that there aren't any pictures of anyone but these four around the place?"

Mal said he had.

"There's one or two other things," said Jarvis, "maybe important, maybe not. They bought the house for cash three years ago. Before that, they lived in Los Angeles. And they were very well off — stocks and shares, and copies of tax returns showing a big income."

"How big?"

"Millionaires."

* * *

"Lots of Johns," Daniel commented when Mal told him all the names from the papers at *Ty Gelli*, "I'll see how many we can find."

He went out into the CID office and found Bethan and Charlie. "I've got a bunch of people we need to try to locate," he said, "the dead couple's parents, and we need everything we can get on the family themselves. Where did the parents work, where did the girls go to school, all that stuff." Mal had emailed pictures of all the documents, and Daniel forwarded them on.

Bethan studied the photographs for a moment. Daniel assumed that she was reflecting on the loss of so much life, but he was wrong.

"John Edwards," she said, waking her computer up. She rattled at the keyboard and turned the monitor towards Daniel. It showed a *Scotsman* article:

Edwards Retires, with a picture of a dark-haired footballer, almost airborne, toe just connecting with the ball, and the goal visible in the corner of the shot.

Charlie and Daniel read the story over Bethan's shoulder. John Edwards had played for Rangers and Scotland, and moved to the USA once his Scottish international days were over. The article announced that he had now retired altogether from football, and planned to return to the UK.

"He looked familiar," she said, "he was pretty well known until a few years ago. Lots of caps for Scotland."

"We wouldn't know," said Charlie, indicating himself and Daniel, "wrong shaped ball."

"No such thing in our house," said Bethan, "Mine would watch ping-pong if that was the only sport on the box. Sports trivia? I'm your girl."

"Wasn't there some kind of scandal?" Charlie asked, "Something to do with sex? Though isn't that every footballer, ever?"

Bethan said that she though it rang a bell, but the heat was fuddling her brain.

"OK," said Daniel, "Bethan you're on John Edwards, Charlie, you do his missus and I'll see what I can find out about the kids. Number one priority is to find the next-of-kin, and the little boy's relatives." That John Edwards had been famous, albeit a few years ago, should make their job easier, though it could also bring the press nosing around, especially if there had been a scandal. Sex and football — nothing the press liked better. Perhaps that's why the family had moved to Gelli, Daniel thought. Because no one would ever find them there. Before he started trying to find out where the girls went to school, he rang Veronica.

She answered and he could hear the background noise of the social services office — endless telephones ringing, people talking and doors slamming — he pictured the chaos of paper files, dusty pot plants and tatty furniture. It didn't make him feel better about the underfunding of the police service, but he knew there were others worse off.

"Is there any chance that the little boy could tell us what happened?" he asked Veronica. "I know that he only has a few words, but could he?"

"Maybe." Veronica sounded thoughtful. "The thing is he might have seen things, but not understood them, so even if he had the words, the events might not make any sense to him. Have you found any relatives yet?"

Daniel told her no, and she told him that the boy was now with a foster carer and out of hospital.

"Stay in touch," she said.

He said he would. Daniel's body still held the imprint of the child, baby warmth and tears like tattoos on his skin.

* * *

Mal had no idea what a millionaire's house ought to look like, but he wouldn't have picked *Ty Gelli* as a contender. It was a nice house, and appeared well loved and well maintained. The furniture was all good quality, and some of it, like the children's beds must have been made just for them. The living room had a big TV, and an expensive sound system. But it didn't shout *millionaire.* No home cinema, no swimming pool. He said as much to Paul Jarvis.

"We haven't looked in the garage yet. Maybe there's a Ferrari or two."

Mal was still suited up, so he went to see.

The garage was attached to the house, and did have an expensive car inside, but it wasn't a Ferrari. Instead, a Range Rover sat on its own. It hadn't been cleaned for a while, and it wasn't the most recent model. It fitted the house. Money, but not millions.

Behind the house, the quarry space had been turned into a garden, with children in mind. The vegetable growing area was at the side, where it would get the most light, but round here there were swings, and a climbing frame. The space was bigger than Mal had expected, with plenty of room to run about. A football had been left by one of the swings, and two pink bicycles leaned up against the back wall of the garage. Next to them a heap of plastic turned out to be an inflatable paddling pool, waiting to be filled with air and water. The smell of cut grass was in the air, and Mal could see that someone had mowed within the last couple of days, with only a few daisy heads starting to show amongst the green. The grass couldn't be called a lawn, but it was neat. Is that how John Edwards had spent his last day? Tidying the paddling pool and mowing the grass, before murdering his family and killing himself? Mal couldn't make it add up.

He walked round to the vegetable garden, recognising the signs of serious growers. A cage covered the soft fruit bushes. Next to the cage, a wheelbarrow held secateurs, a trowel and a garden fork. Raised beds had vegetables interspersed with flowers — what Daniel called 'companion planting'. *The things I know.* Everything looked healthy and as if the gardeners had gone inside for a cup of tea, leaving their tools ready to pick up and resume work. A neat shed held seed packets, pots, compost, tomato food, string and tools hung up on hooks above a potting bench. Whoever the gardener was, he or she had expected to be back.

He returned to the house and Paul Jarvis.

"I need to start interviewing the neighbours," he said, "Is there anything else I should see before I go?"

"Nothing to see, but something else odd. We haven't found any mobile phones."

"They weren't on the bodies?"

"No. Not in any of the obvious places. They do exist, because there are bills, but the actual phones aren't here. Or if they are, they're well hidden. I've tried ringing the numbers, but nothing."

* * *

A call to the Local Education Authority produced the information that the Edwards sisters were not registered at any of the local schools. Daniel asked if there were any private schools within daily driving distance of Gelli, and got the name of the only one. The School Secretary of St Margaret's (Independent) School didn't want to talk to him, but he wore her down, only to find that the girls had not been pupils there either.

"Homeschooled," said Bethan, when he told her, "check if there are any local homeschooling groups."

An internet search revealed that north east Wales had a lot of homeschoolers, so Daniel started telephoning. It was a task he could have given to someone else, but he couldn't forget the feeling of Dafydd crying snottily onto his chest, smelling the baby smell of him, and that sudden grin at the hospital, and he wanted to make things right for the little boy, as if by doing so he could make things right for himself.

The homeschoolers were friendly enough, friendlier than Daniel had expected, but none of them had anything useful to say. He'd had to leave messages for two, and as he ended his list, one of them — a woman called Willow — rang back.

"Edwards, yes, two little girls, and their mother, Hayley was it?"

Daniel said that it was.

"They only came a couple of times," said Willow, "maybe three times. Then last year she said she'd got a group together with her neighbours. They were nice, but it's a long drive, so something local made more sense."

"Did they ever bring a baby? A little boy? Or mention him?" Daniel asked.

"If they did, I don't remember," Willow replied. Willow didn't have much more to tell. Hayley and the girls had only been to the group a few times, and the children had mostly taken the chance to play with the others. There had been some storytelling, a bit of reading and writing, and probably a nature walk.

"Because that's what we do. I don't remember anything special about those days." Daniel asked about what Hayley had said about the group with her neighbours, but Willow had nothing to add. Just *neighbours*.

There was a knock at the door and Charlie came in.

"Bad news about Hayley Edwards's parents, boss. Both dead. Cancer, five years apart. John Patterson died last year."

"Did she have any brothers or sisters?" Daniel asked.

"Nope. But I can go looking for aunts, uncles, grandparents, if you like."

Daniel told him to see what he could find. Maybe Bethan would have a bit more luck. He went out to see.

"You want the good news or the bad news?" she asked.

"Good, please."

"John Edwards senior and Marian Edwards are both still alive. The bad news is that they aren't answering the phone. All I've got is a landline and an address in Worcester. I've left a message."

"Brothers and sisters?"

"A sister, Catherine. Also lives in Worcester, also not answering the phone."

Bethan's desk phone rang. She listened for a moment and said,

"I already told him the DCI won't be back for hours, and yes, I did leave a note." She listened again. "He can keep coming back. It won't change anything."

Daniel raised his eyebrows. Bethan put the phone down.

"Some young bloke wants to see the DCI. He was here before you got back from Gelli, and judging from that, is going to keep coming until he gets what he wants, whatever that is. Nice-looking boy."

Daniel smiled. "Not sure I want nice-looking boys hanging around my bloke, leaving notes," he said.

Bethan smiled back. "It's on his desk. You could ring the number and warn him off. Jamie Maddocks his name is."

"Oh, shit." Daniel said. "Just what we don't need."

It was Bethan's turn to raise her eyebrows.

"You remember when the DCI first came here?" Bethan nodded. "And do you remember how there was all that gossip about how he wasn't a team player, or a good colleague?" Bethan nodded again. "Well, Ethan Maddocks was a rent boy who killed himself after he was raped by a police officer in the cells. Everyone knew who the rapist was, but they were going to let him off with a reprimand. The DCI wouldn't let it drop."

"I think you told me at the time," Bethan said.

"Probably. I told a lot of people. What I didn't tell you was that the rapist and his mates put Mal in hospital. Waited for him in a car park and beat him up. Only Mal had a body-cam and recorded it all."

"No more talk of reprimands?"

"All sacked, and the rapist went to prison."

"Which is why the DCI came here."

"Just so," said Daniel, "don't blame the criminal, drive the whistle-blower out of town."

"So you're worried that this Jamie Maddocks is something to to with Ethan Maddocks?"

"Wouldn't you be?"

Because there's something about that boy's death that Mal can't escape.

Chapter 5

O ver the course of his life, he had learned that no one could be trusted, or not for long. No one was what they seemed, no one.

Hector had suspected for some time that Sasha had more energy than ordinary mortals, but even he was surprised to get home and find the front garden weeded, the lawn at the back mowed, and Sasha and Arwen sitting on a blanket eating sandwiches. He waved at them from the back door and went to shower. Once he felt clean enough to be with other humans, he went outside and hugged them both.

"Not all fun and glamour, your job then?" Sasha asked, knowing the answer.

"Not this morning."

He helped himself to sandwiches and had taken the first bite when he saw the cake. "Don't tell me you made cake too?"

"OK, I won't."

"Mama made cake." Arwen said, "and I helped."

"Helped clean the bowl anyway," said Sasha.

"Would you like to marry me?" Hector said.

Sasha laughed. "Be careful," she said, "I might start taking you seriously."

How do you know I'm not serious? I think I might be. Because I've never felt like this about anyone else, man or woman.

He wasn't interested in gardening, though the size and privacy of the garden had been one of the reasons that he bought the cottage. The previous owners had laid a good foundation, and with a bit of help from Daniel, he'd managed to keep it from getting away from him. But he'd never sat on a rug on the lawn before, eating homemade cake and watching a small girl look for the fairies her mother insisted could be found in the laurel bushes.

The dead children in Gelli were dimming the sunshine in his day, but he wasn't going to let them spoil everyone's weekend.

"Still fancy the beach?" he asked Sasha, "If you don't, there's a couple of good walks."

"Walk," she said, "all the beaches will be packed. We need to wear Arwen out, and running round the garden won't do it."

"Five miles? She's only got little legs."

"It's a start. Listen, I answered your landline while you were out. Well strictly speaking, Arwen answered it, and I took it off her. Someone who sounded like the queen asked for you, and wanted to know who I was. I said I was staying here, and that you were at work. Gotta say, I don't think she was impressed."

* * *

The elderly man at the first house wanted to be as unhelpful as he had been earlier. Even now that Mal was now dressed professionally, and had his warrant card, and an equally professional-looking Abby Price by his side, the man didn't want to let them in. At the same time, he wanted to know what was going on, why there were police cars filling the road. Curiosity won the day, and in they went.

Once inside, Mal wasn't sure he wouldn't have preferred to stay on the doorstep. The house reeked of old food, dirty clothes, cat litter, and an uncleaned bathroom. The living room opened straight off the street, and although superficially tidy, was coated in dust and cobwebs. Despite the warm day, a dangerously ancient gas fire hissed in the fireplace, heating the odours to nausea -inducing levels. A long haired cat slept on the sofa. Judging by the layer of fur, the cat had been in possession of the sofa for some time. Mal made a mental note to call social services. They weren't invited to sit down, which was a relief.

Mal introduced himself and Abby again, and asked for the man's name.

"James Protheroe. Welsh Guards. Retired." Mal thought *never mind social services, the army should be helping this man.*

"Then, sir, I expect you must be a good observer." Mal said, "What can you tell me about your next door neighbours?"

"The hippies or the footballer?"

"Both. But perhaps you could start with the Edwardses? Anything happen over the last couple of days?"

Protheroe's expression was calculating, as if he was deciding how much to reveal. "They didn't let their chickens out this morning," he said. "They wander all over the road and get into my garden, nasty things."

"What about yesterday and last night?"

"He was in the garden, offered to cut my grass, as if I'm too decrepit to use a mower. She was out too, and those girls were running about yelling."

"That was a normal day then?"

Protheroe nodded.

"And nothing unusual in the evening?"

"I watched the idiot box and went to bed. Slept the same as usual, clear conscience, see. Then some silly bugger woke me up banging at the door." He poked his finger at Mal. "Half dressed, claiming to be a copper. Funniest looking copper I ever saw." He giggled, and Mal smiled.

"It's not the way I usually dress for work, sir. So you didn't hear anything in the night?"

"That's what I just said."

"Yes, sir, you did." Mal was aware of the hearing aids, and assumed that Protheroe removed them to sleep. It was possible that he hadn't heard three gunshots if he'd been in bed when they were fired.

"What time did you go to sleep, Mr Protheroe? Roughly"

"I get the ten o'clock headlines and go upstairs," he said, "unless there's something new. Last night there wasn't."

That either meant that the shots weren't fired until, say ten fifteen, or Protheroe had been watching something on the TV with lots of noise.

"What did you watch on the TV before the news?" he asked, hoping it wouldn't be a war film.

Protheroe looked embarrassed. "I couldn't tell you. I put it on, see, and nine times out of ten I drop off and wake up five minutes before the news. The joy of old age. It's no good."

* * *

"I think we'll have to ask Worcester if they'll send someone round." Daniel said. "We need to identify the bodies, and the next of kin need to know." *And if Dafydd is the Edwards's son, they'll be his nearest relatives, maybe his only relatives.* He told Charlie to keep looking for Hayley's family, and went to find a number for Worcester police.

A cheerful sergeant promised to arrange a call to the senior Edwardses straight away, "and we'll have a chat to the neighbours if they aren't there, find out if anyone's got a number." But when he rang back, it wasn't with good news.

"They're away on a cruise. No one's got their number, and no one knows where they've gone. Just a chat while they were putting the bins out. The daughter has gone with them, and none of her neighbours has a number for *her* either." The parents lived on a street of big houses where people kept to themselves, and the daughter in a block of flats where people were out at work all day.

"Facebook, then," said Charlie.

"Ring the cruise companies, and the Border Agency," said Bethan.

"Sorry," said Daniel, "get started and I'll go and ask the Super for some more people to help us."

Bethan went to set up the Incident Room while a civilian researcher made lists of cruise company phone numbers, and Charlie groused his way through the hundreds of people called Catherine Edwards on social media. Daniel rang Mal.

"How's it going?" he asked.

"Slowly. We've only this minute been able to let the adults' bodies go. I'm going to have to mess up the rest of Hector's long week with Sasha, and ask him to do the autopsies tomorrow. The old bloke claims to have slept the sleep of the just last night, oblivious to three gunshots in the next house."

Daniel told Mal what Willow had said about homeschooling with the neighbours. "Which doesn't mean there is a homeschooling group ..."

"I haven't asked, but I wouldn't be surprised. There are lots of kids. Bit of a hippy commune vibe."

"Beard prejudice, Maldwyn?"

"Maybe. I'll tell you when I've spoken to them properly. I want to bring Paul Jarvis in for the briefing, but the CSI team will have to come back tomorrow. They've got to take the house to pieces."

Daniel told Mal about their so far unsuccessful attempt to find any Edwards relatives, and that John Edwards had been a well known footballer. Except he already knew that.

"One of the CSI's recognised his picture. Only we don't know that our DB *is* John Edwards."

"I'll see if I can find John Edwards's doctor, maybe someone from the football days. Because we aren't going to get an ID from his face, and dental records won't work. If there were any injuries, Hector can look for them. I've already checked our records. Neither of them had so much as a parking ticket."

Daniel thought about whether to mention the note from Jamie Maddocks and decided not to. They had enough to deal with.

* * *

"Well at least he didn't offer us a drink, sir," said Abby, when they were breathing the fresh air again, outside the old man's house, and Mal had ended his call, "I wouldn't offend the old guy, but I couldn't have stayed in there much longer,"

Mal didn't answer, but he thought he'd be putting his clothes in the wash as soon as he got home. He made a note on his phone to find out if there was a welfare service for ex-Welsh Guards.

"See if you can find out what was on the telly last night before the news," he said, "The main channels, I don't think he's got anything else. The DI left a flask — I'll get us both a drink."

While he was pouring coffee for himself and Abby, hoping she took it black and sugarless, he phoned Bethan.

"Could you get someone to bring some cold drinks and sandwiches over? We're going to be here all day."

Bethan said she'd get it organised. He wondered about bringing the incident van, but a decision could wait until they'd spoken to more of the neighbours.

Abby was looking at the TV schedules on her phone. She looked at the coffee, and said thank you. From her demeanour, Mal guessed that black and sugarless wasn't her brew of choice, but the weather was hot, and they needed to drink.

"Friday night TV isn't very big on excitement," she said. "Nothing that would cover gunshots anyway, though I expect he'd have it on loud because of his hearing."

"So tentatively, no shots until after the news started," said Mal, "Let's hope we get something more definite from the others."

The next house in the terrace was the one where Mal had seen everyone gather earlier on. The door was painted bright yellow, and there were pots of marigolds on either side of the step. The windows sparkled in the sun. He could hear voices inside the house, and the noise of children playing — outbursts of laughter, then cries of 'not fair', and the sound of an older child giving instructions in a bossy voice. He'd grown up with with five siblings and he recognised the pattern.

"Ready?" he asked Abby, and they put their empty cups on the ground by the step, to collect on their way out, and knocked on the door. It was opened by the woman Mal had seen earlier talking to Daniel. She had been carrying a baby, he remembered, but not now.

He showed her his warrant card and introduced himself and Abby, and she stood aside to let them in.

The whole of the downstairs of the house had been knocked into one big space. Too big, in fact. Mal saw that they were standing in a space made from the downstairs of this house, and the one next door, with a doorway into the third house. This side of the room held sofas and easy chairs, and the rear of the house was a big kitchen and a huge table. He noticed two high chairs pulled up to the table, as well as chairs with cushions to raise the seats for bigger children. *Communal living? Or a big family?*

A man stepped forwards. He had a long beard, plaited with coloured threads, and hair to match. His feet were bare and grubby, as if he'd come in from the garden. He held out his hand.

"Mabon ap Richard," he said, "how can we help?"

* * *

The afternoon ground on, the combination of computers pouring out heat and acres of glass raising the temperature inside the police station, until they were too hot, even with rolled up sleeves and all the fans they could find. At least they could find fans, Daniel thought, because they weren't finding much information.

The civilian researcher was steadily ringing the big cruise companies, amassing information, but not finding the Edwards family.

"The Border Agency are supposed to be getting back to me," she said, "but they are as short staffed as we are."

Charlie had found three possible Catherine Edwardses on social media, and had sent them all messages. But if the family *was* on a cruise, their access to the internet would be restricted and expensive.

None of the Edwards family, nor anyone else from Gelli, had a license for any kind of gun, and a sawn off shotgun was illegal regardless. Melin Tywyll had a shooting club, and Daniel knew several of its members were in the police. He spoke to them all. None of them had any knowledge of anyone from Gelli, and none of them had heard of a sawn off shotgun in the area.

The only positive result was that Daniel was able to contact both

Rangers Football Club, and the club John Edwards had played for in the USA. Full sets of medical records were being emailed. Edwards hadn't broken any bones, but he'd had some torn muscles and damaged cartilage, so Daniel hoped that something would have left a mark for Hector to find. Which meant that Daniel had to ask Hector to take another chunk out of his week to do the autopsy.

"Don't worry," Hector said, "as soon as I saw the male body, I knew I'd be in tomorrow."

Daniel apologised again for the loss of Hector's time with Sasha. Hector cleared his throat.

"She's OK. Something I want to tell you. After the autopsy?"

Daniel agreed, puzzled, because the romance between Sasha and Hector had seemed to be going well.

"You OK, mate?" he asked.

"I'll talk to you about it tomorrow." And that was the only answer he got.

Mal sent over a list of the names of the Gelli residents, and they began to find out what they could about them all.

The first name in the list came with a big star and the comment: *this guy isn't real!*

Mabon ap Richard didn't exist anywhere in their records, including on the electoral register. A Michael Richardson *was* registered at number four Gelli Terrace, and Michael Richardson *did* have a record — a long list of criminal damage, breach of the peace, trespass, assault on a police officer. Richardson was an environmental protestor, though he hadn't been arrested since moving to Wales. Prior to moving house to Gelli, Richardson had lived in Devon, and had travelled all over the country, chaining himself to fences and sleeping in trees. But three years ago, it had all ended. The last mention of Richardson was as part of a call out to a 'disturbance' at the house in Devon where he lived. The address was Holyoak Hall, and the report referred to it as an *intentional community.* Daniel picked up the phone to find out more.

Chapter 6

H e thought of all the decisions he'd made in his life, all the changes, the things he'd done to try to escape the past. At every point someone let him down.

Mal had taken an instant and visceral dislike to Mabon ap Richard. Everything about him shouted *Fake!* Mal knew that he was obsessive about his own personal hygiene, and about his clothes and the way he looked. He thought that Mabon was the same, only he didn't want anyone to know. Mal thought this man wanted to project the image of someone who is above worrying about appearance, by deliberately wearing slightly grubby clothes, and letting his feet become encrusted with dirt. The coloured threads in his hair and beard were designed to show that he was free and easy, without any hang ups about traditional masculinity. *I bet he calls himself a feminist, and hits on every woman who comes his way.* He was certainly giving Abby a not very subtle appraisal.

"Thank you Mr ap Richard," Mal said, "We're obviously here about a serious incident at your neighbours' house. We have some questions, but I wonder if we could start with some names?"

"Mabon, please. Can you tell us what happened?"

"We don't know yet," Mal said, "that's why we're here." Nothing about his words, or body language betrayed his irritation.

The woman, Mel, who had let them in stepped forward.

"Please come and sit down," she said, "and can we get you a drink? Mint tea?"

Mal said that would be very nice, thank you, and everyone shuffled round, leaving a small sofa for himself and Abby. Mal could still hear the children shouting and playing, and as Mel went to boil the kettle, the back door crashed open and a boy of about ten ran in demanding drinks for everyone. Mel ushered him back out, with the promise of drinks and biscuits in half an hour — if they kept the noise down. She came back with a tray of mugs and a big teapot.

"I'll leave it for a minute," she said, "Names, then. I'm Mel Ward, Mabon's partner, and three of the monsters out there are mine." She looked to her right, to another long-haired woman, sitting with her feet curled up underneath her, leaning on a man with a rusty coloured beard, and a shaven head. She looked tired. "Bethany Hall," she said, "sorry if I'm a bit dopey, we've got a baby and she's not sleeping through yet. This is my husband Tom." The final couple introduced themselves as Cai and Becca Jones.

Mel poured the tea, and handed it around, clear and green in the mugs, made with handfuls of fresh mint, stuffed into the teapot. Mal thought that it smelled wonderful. He wasn't sure that Abby felt the same.

"You're bound to be wondering," Mel said, "we converted the houses so that we can share the kitchen and eat together."

"We believe in sharing," Mabon said, "raising the children in a community, helping them to find common ground with each other and with us. Humans aren't made to be closed off into exclusive groups, living to consume more and more."

Complete and utter bullshit, thought Mal, but he kept his expression warm and supportive.

"Were the Edwards family part of your community?" he asked.

* * *

Holyoak Hall had a website, and it looked fabulous. The pictures were of an arts and crafts manor in beautiful grounds, lots of trees, a lake and enough fruit and veg to supply a small town. The blurbs described *living in a community of like-minded people,* and *being the change you want to see.* Away from the hype, the Hall residents aimed for self-sufficiency, consensus decision-making, and lots of shared cooking, eating and work. Reading between the lines, it was clear that maintaining the house required constant labour, and there was a desperate need for people who had more than basic DIY skills. There was only one kitchen, and all the bathrooms were shared, so residents had to be willing to live communally, as well as to take part in regular house meetings, and take turns cooking, washing up and cleaning. The sub-text was *no slackers.* Some residents had jobs, others didn't, but all were expected to contribute their labour and some cash.

If this was where Michael Richardson had lived, he was unlikely to get a quick answer to his questions by ringing the number on the website. Instead he rang the local police.

"It's reported as a *disturbance.* You arrested Michael Richardson and a couple of others," Daniel told his opposite number in Devon. "Michael Richardson has come up in a case here, and I'm looking for background."

"They're nice people at the Hall, for all that they're forever protesting about something. I can't tell you much about your bloke, but I know the rest of them didn't like him. I've got a couple of numbers you could try." One was the same number as the website, the other was a mobile number for a Jay Grieve. "She's the one who comes in to liaise about demonstrations and so on. She's been there since the start."

Daniel rang the mobile number, and a woman with a rich, deep voice and an accent like Hector's answered. Daniel explained who he was and what he wanted. "Michael, or Mabon, as he's called now, isn't being accused of anything," he said, "he's a close neighbour of the victim of a serious crime. It's a very small community and we're trying to find out everything we can about the people who live there. We know he was very politically active until he left Holyoak Hall, and we know that he was arrested after a disturbance at the Hall."

There was a long silence at the other end of the line.

"Ms Grieve?" Daniel asked.

"I'm walking and thinking," she said, "wait."

Daniel waited.

"People think that communal living is all lentils and casual sex. It isn't. It's hard work. Physical and emotional. We are trying to live in an entirely different way, to prove that there is a better life than pointless work and shopping, and that's never going to be easy. But the rewards are incredible. Making connections with other people, building a community, being authentic, knowing that you are a small part of the solution to what ails the world."

She paused again, but only for a moment.

"But that makes us vulnerable, both as a community and as individuals. People here want to see the best in others. We try to be open to others, to see things through their eyes, rather than to judge by our own prejudices. It takes a long time to join a community like ours — time spent volunteering, joining our work weeks, observing meetings, being interviewed. We need to know that people who join are serious about what we are trying to do.

"So once a person has joined, we find it hard to admit that we have made a mistake. We distrust our reactions, make excuses, because surely no one could convince us all that they were sincere and committed, when really they were a sexual predator, a liar and a manipulator. We should have seen through the lies before, so we don't believe our eyes now. It can take a long time to see through the charm to the nastiness underneath. And then you can lose all confidence in your own judgement.

"The nearest analogy I have is the way the police infiltrated protest groups. Such people do a lot of damage.

"And that's all I have to say. Goodbye Detective Inspector."

* * *

"John and Hayley weren't ready to share living space, but they did share many of our ideas and our values." Mabon said, "I think of them as part of our community." He looked round at the others and they all nodded. Mal thought Mabon could bore for Wales about 'values', but Abby appeared *interested.*

"We love the girls, as much as any of the others," said Mel, "and the little one too." Again, everyone else nodded, eyes shining. Mal thought the nodding was automatic, as if everyone was used to agreeing with whatever Mabon said. It was over-enthusiastic, designed to convince him of their sincerity.

Mal asked what activities the households shared, given that they weren't sharing living space. Mabon answered before anyone else could speak, although he thought, no one else was rushing to say anything anyway.

"We all worked together in the gardens, and the children are all homeschooled, so Seren and Stella joined in there. Hayley was great at science, and took a bit of a lead."

"Did they come and eat with you?" Mal asked, thinking of the dining table at *Ty Gelli*, covered in children's things. There was a table in the kitchen, but it would seat a small family, not this whole group.

"Fairly often," said Mabon, but from the body language of the rest of

49

the group, Mal thought *not very often* was nearer the mark.

"What's *happened to them?*" Becca cried, "We're all sitting here as if we haven't seen police there all day, and no sign of John or Hayley or the girls. *Tell us, please.*"

Mal thought that even this pleading sounded false, but he worried that his prejudices were leading him astray. He knew that what had happened would be public knowledge soon enough. Maybe someone in this room had played a role in the deaths, but Mal was certain that they all knew their neighbours wouldn't be coming home. He also noticed that Becca, like Mel had referred to *John, Hayley and the girls.* No mention of the baby, even as an afterthought. He looked at the big room and the people in it. Whatever the truth of the Edwards's commitment to communal living, their deaths were going cause shockwaves, not least to the children. But the Edwards family had a right to know first.

"We don't know what happened," he said, "I can tell you that we found the bodies of a number of people in your neighbours' house. Until we have formally identified those bodies, we aren't in a position to give names. I'm sorry."

Becca burst into noisy tears, burying her face in her husband's shoulder. Bethany said "Not the girls, please, not the girls." Tom stood up and went to the back door.

"I'm going to watch the children," he said, and left. Bethany jumped up and ran after him.

"I realise this must be a terrible shock," said Mal, still wondering if it was, "but I do have a couple more questions, things we need to know urgently."

"Of course," said Mabon, extending his hand as if graciously granting permission for Mal to do his job. He felt Abby stir beside him, heard her dislike of Mabon, though she was silent and looking down at her notebook.

"Did anything unusual happen yesterday? Did you see or speak to your neighbours?"

It had been a normal day everyone said. They had played with the children, worked in the gardens, been for walks, had dinner, gone to bed.

"Did you watch television?" Mal asked.

"We don't have one." came the inevitable answer.

* * *

As the time ticked towards the briefing at five o'clock, the frustration in the CID office grew. Both John and Hayley Edwards had been good citizens, and whilst their young neighbours had a selection of breaches of the peace, and obstruction of the highway charges in their records, there was nothing to indicate this level of violence. Sure, Jay Grieve had all but told Daniel that Michael Richardson was an untrustworthy snake in the grass, and an exploiter of women. But did that make him a murderer?

James Protheroe was exactly what he said he was — a retired NCO from the Welsh Guards. It had taken some persuasion to get the army to release the information, but Sergeant Protheroe had been honourably discharged at the end of a long career. After retirement, he'd worked as a groundsman at Melin Tywyll Golf Club, but there was no one around who remembered him.

The terrace has five houses Daniel thought. James Protheroe in the one closest to Ty Gelli, then the three communal houses, so who lives in the last one? He looked out of his office. Everyone was staring at their computers and scribbling notes. He brought up the Land Registry site himself, beginning with *Ty Gelli*. No surprise, it was owned by John and Hayley Edwards.

As were numbers one to five, Gelli Terrace. They had owned all of it.

Daniel sent Mal a text, and got a call.

"I'm on my way back. None of them said that they paid rent to Edwards. I assumed they owned their homes." Mal described the way that the houses had been knocked into one — not something most landlords would agree to.

"We just have to hope that the records are in Edwards's house," Mal said.

At a quarter to five Veronica called to see if they'd had any luck locating Dafydd's relatives. "At this point," Daniel said, "I'm not even sure he's called Dafydd."

"The foster carer says he responds to it, as if it's his name, but he's not happy, keeps asking for Dada and Mum, poor little thing."

"There's no birth certificate at the house for him, but the neighbours say he lived there. Sorry, Vee, we are trying." He couldn't help thinking of the little boy, walking on his own, in his wellies and T-shirt. If he wasn't Hayley and John's son, who was he?

* * *

Jamie Maddocks went back to the Police station for the third time. The little town was very sweet, he thought, but he'd spent long enough in the cafes, and looked exhaustively in every shop. He now owned a rather lovely new silk scarf, but the only shop left to be explored was the farmer's co-op. Looking through the window, he thought that it might be quite interesting, if he wanted bags of animal feed, a five-bar gate, or even a coal scuttle. But as his usual accommodation was half a small ship's cabin, maybe not. If he couldn't see Kent this time, he'd find a bed and breakfast, and spend the evening with some videos. From what his cousin had told him, the detective *would* talk to him, and he had plenty of time before he had to be back in Southampton.

When he got to the glass building behind the car park, he saw a handsome, very dark man getting out of a police car. There were other people in the car, but Jamie was sure the dark man was his quarry. He looked like the policeman his mother had described as asking about Ethan. "The only one who seemed to care," she had said. He was even more sure when the man looked up and saw him. His mother's house was full of photographs of Jamie, and of Ethan.

"I'll catch you up," Jamie heard the man say to his companions.

"Mr Kent?" Jamie asked. He'd never been clear about titles.

"DCI Maldwyn Kent," said the man, "and you must be related to Ethan Maddocks."

"Jamie Maddocks, Ethan's cousin. I've come to talk to you about some things Ethan told me. I've been away — I work on cruise ships. I got back and Ethan had left me a letter."

DCI Kent took Jamie's arm and led him to a bench next to the door to the police station. Judging by the number of cigarette butts on the ground, it was the smoking corner. Jamie's gaydar was pinging loudly. OK the policeman was forty (at least) but he was a gorgeous bear of a man. Jamie's mother hadn't mentioned *that*, but why would she? Ethan himself had only met Kent once, and he'd been suicidal at the time, but he said the man had been kind. Things were looking up. Only not for long. The door opened and a tall, thin, blond man put his head out. Jamie's gaydar pinged again. Not his type, but no question about this one's sexuality. Or about the way he looked at Kent.

"Mal?" the blond guy said.

"Five minutes. This is Ethan Maddocks' cousin Jamie."

Jamie saw a shadow pass over the blond man's face, but he smiled. "Hi Jamie." He looked at Kent. "I'll get you a coffee. Seriously, don't be long."

"Is everyone here gay?" Jamie asked without thinking, *because come on, rural police station in north Wales?*

Kent smiled, but Jamie didn't think it went all the way through. "No," he said, "and that isn't important. I've got a major case on, you'll see it in the news. I don't have time to talk today."

"I'll wait. I'm going to find somewhere to stay. I need to tell you what Ethan said."

"Give me your number. I've got to go. Sorry. I'll ring as soon as I can but it won't be till late."

The minute he had Jamie's phone number, Kent disappeared into the police station.

Chapter 7

*O*nly the children are truly innocent, he thought. But one day they will turn into monsters, like all the rest. It's already started.

Never mind Jamie Maddocks, concentrate on Dafydd Edwards. Daniel needed to keep his head in the game and not let it wander off thinking about what might go wrong. The anxiety rose in his throat, threatening to close it and stop his breathing. It had been happening more often since the night in the Burns and Wood building in Manchester. A sudden spike of worry that he wouldn't cope. He'd had to be violent, horribly violent, and two men had died. He hadn't killed either of them, but he couldn't forget that Andy Carter's last minutes of life had been spent in pain and fear, and that he, Daniel, was responsible. He shook his head to banish the images, forcing himself to picture the little boy's smile in the hospital that morning.

Knowing that Dafydd was safe and cared for was a start, but Daniel hated to think that the boy was missing his parents, whoever they were. Daniel thought that he wouldn't be the only one wondering whether John and Hayley Edwards weren't Dafydd's parents. If that were true, the child might get his family back, but then ... the thoughts fluttered, unformed, making no connections or patterns, until Mal came upstairs and they could start the briefing.

Superintendent Hart walked to the front of the room. She didn't expect people to stand up, but everyone straightened in their chairs.

"This may be the worst case I've ever had to deal with," she said, "but I know that we are doing the right things to find out what happened in that house last night. At the moment, we're ahead of the press, but that won't last. I don't want these people's families to find out from the internet that their loved ones are dead. So please, as we go through what we know, if you have an idea, share it."

She turned to Mal, who projected pictures of the scene in the kitchen, and the two girls' bodies, showed a plan of the six houses, and summarised what Hector had said.

"Dr Lord thinks that the two girls were smothered, probably with a pillow. They were left tucked up in bed as if they were sleeping. In the kitchen, the woman's body is almost certainly Hayley Edwards." Mal showed a picture of Hayley, smiling, with her arms around her daughters. "The assumption is that the dead man is her husband, but as yet we haven't been able to identify him. The assumption is also that this is the killing of a family by the father and husband, who then killed himself. It's the most likely scenario. But so far we haven't proved that the dead man wasn't a victim himself, and that the gun was put touching his hand after he was dead.

"There is the added complication of the child DI Owen and I found this morning outside the house. Neighbours suggested that this child belonged to the Edwards family. But there are documents in the house for the two girls, nothing for the boy."

Mal quickly outlined their interviews with Mabon and the other people in their group, plus James Protheroe, and turned to Daniel.

"We've been trying to contact the Edwards's next of kin." Daniel said, "Hayley was an only child and her parents are both dead. We're looking for anyone else. John's parents are alive, as is his sister. Unfortunately, they are away, and we're struggling to locate them, or even get their mobile numbers." He looked at Superintendent Hart. "The Border Agency are supposed to be calling us back, but nothing yet."

Hart nodded. "Leave it with me."

Daniel told them about the Edwards's ownership of all the houses in Gelli. Paul Jarvis chimed in with the information that the family had been very rich.

"So who gets the money?" Charlie Rees asked.

"The wills we found were made a long time ago," said Jarvis, "they leave the money to each other, and then their children, with John's sister appointed to look after them. John Patterson, Hayley's father is mentioned as one of the executors, and he died over a year ago. If the little boy is their child, then he will inherit, otherwise the sister. But we'd need to double check. And check that there isn't another will somewhere else."

There was a moment's silence as they all reflected.

Paul Jarvis said, "We've got the name of the solicitor who made the wills, and the estate agent and solicitor who handled the house purchase."

Bethan was making notes for follow-up actions. Both solicitors would need visits.

"We've been looking at the neighbours," said Daniel, "though that was before we knew they were all the Edwards's tenants. James Protheroe is exactly who he says he is, a retired Sargeant in the Welsh Guards. Can't find out anything to his detriment.

"Mabon ap Richard has changed his name from Michael Richardson, and he has a record for lots of offences related to environmental protests. He lived in an intentional community in Devon, until three years ago, and I spoke to a founder member. She implied very strongly that Richardson was a liar and a sexual predator, and that they were glad to get rid of him.

"The rest of the group have similar records for environmental protests, nothing serious, but so far that's all we know about any of them."

"There's another house," said Abby, "who lives there? We knocked, but no one answered."

Daniel had to say that they didn't know.

Superintendent Hart asked about the boy Dafydd. Mal said that the identification had come from Mel Ward, first thing in the morning.

"But, sir," Abby said, "when we were talking to them this afternoon, they kept mentioning the little girls, and only adding the boy in later." Mal nodded.

Jarvis said, "We found a nursery in the Edwards's house though it didn't look used. And when we looked at the car, it had no child seat, and there was no sign of one anywhere on the premises."

"The hospital said that Dafydd wasn't injured, and had been well cared for," said Daniel, "If the family died yesterday evening, and he was part of the family, where was he until we found him?"

The next question came from an unexpected source.

"If the baby isn't Dafydd Edwards, was he kidnapped? Shouldn't we be searching for missing children?" PC Jones had expected to be spending the night guarding *Ty Gelli*, not invited to the briefing, and he didn't expect to be asking a question, but he'd had all day to think. He didn't believe in the paranormal, and babies don't appear from nowhere. Someone must be missing the child. He saw Sergeant Davies scribbling in her notebook and blushed hard. Then the DCI nodded.

"Good point, Jones. Thanks. And if PC Jones is right, why did the neighbours say he was Dafydd Edwards?"

"I've spoken to the social worker," said Daniel, "and she says that the boy probably is called Dafydd, or rather that he responds to the name, but the co-ordinator of the homeschooling group Hayley went to a couple of times, never saw a baby, and that was only last year."

Mal summed up, turning to Hart for the final word. He knew it wouldn't have any effect, but they had to go through the motions.

"Once the press get wind of this," she said, "our job will get a hundred times harder. The longer we keep quiet, the longer we can investigate in peace. It's up to you. Don't gossip."

It was already too late. The Press Office from force HQ had left messages for Hart and Mal before the briefing was over.

"We need a roadblock Ma'am," said Daniel, "Gelli is at the end of a road to nowhere." Hart nodded.

"I'll sort that out, and put a rocket up the Border Agency's arse. No surprise, but the Chief Constable will be fronting the press conference in the morning, which is good. He's brilliant at saying nothing. And I've organised a pizza delivery. It should be at the front desk in," she looked at the time, "about fifteen minutes."

Hart didn't join them for pizza, but when they had eaten enough to take a pause, uniformed Inspector Sophie Harrington did, abandoning yet another healthy eating attempt.

"I only came to say that the road block is being set up now." she said, pizza triangle in hand, "Looking at the map, there are plenty of paths to Gelli, but only one road. I've spoken to the farmer at the far end of the Gelli road, and he's more than happy to keep an eye open for anyone he doesn't know."

By the time the pizza had all gone, Hart rang to say that the Border Agency would be ringing back with information in the next half an hour.

"I'll take these boxes down to the bin," Daniel said, gathering them all up, and standing on them to squash them flat. He wasn't surprised that Mal followed, or that once the boxes were in the cardboard recycling, Mal pulled him over to the smokers' bench and put an arm round his shoulders. Daniel rolled his shirt sleeves down, and then rolled them up again, trying to get them straight. Then he re-laced his shoes, and tried to flatten his hair. Images of baby Dafydd in the road alone flipped

59

on an endless carousel with images of Andy Carter's death.

"I've been on my feet all day, and I feel like an old man." Mal said after a while.

"Sorry, *cariad*, you'll have to make do with me." Daniel said, and got a weary smile in return. He reached over and stroked Mal's cheek, feeling the day's stubble against his fingers, and then squeezed Mal's hand. "It's been crap."

"Are you OK, love?" Mal asked, worried by Daniel's fidgeting.

"Fine, honestly."

Daniel leaned against Mal, the connection between their bodies warming him, in the way that he had warmed Dafydd. His pulse slowed, and the anxiety receded.

The conversation began, in fits and starts, along the lines of *hard to hear, but better to know*. The smoker's bench caught the evening sun, and it was warm with trees shining in their early summer green on the hills beyond the town. Mal told Daniel about the bodies in the house, the girls' bodies tucked into their beds, and the destruction of Hayley and the male body they were assuming was John. He described the house, how it was full of the children's lives, and the garden, with its fruit and vegetables, bikes and swings.

Daniel glanced over at Mal, and saw the tears again. "It was all so *normal*, not a millionaire's home, or the home of a mad person, just a home. Like your sister's. Or like ours would be if we had kids."

"Hey," he said, taking Mal's hand and stroking his hair, "hey, Maldwyn, it'll be OK." Mal's body was stiff.

"It won't. It's never going to be OK again for those children."

Daniel pulled Mal as close as he could. He wiped Mal's tears with his fingers, and kissed him gently.

"I hate this job sometimes," he said, though he was starting to think he hated it all the time now. "It's always up to us to clean up the mess."

"That must be why we get the big money," Mal said, trying for a smile.

Daniel kissed him again, and Mal kissed him back, and it changed from comfort into something rougher and more urgent. Daniel pushed his fingers under Mal's jacket, feeling the nipple ring through his shirt. He felt Mal's hand on his thigh and ached with the desire to be closer. Buried in Mal, all worry would be silent.

"Fuck." Mal said, pulling away, though not moving his hand. "Where did that come from?" Daniel felt his own skin flushing and saw the colour in Mal's neck and face. Mal's hand caressed Daniel's thigh, moving upwards under its own volition. Daniel's body moved automatically towards it.

"This is how people get sacked," he said, but he kissed Mal again.

"Later," Mal said when they took a breath.

"Promise?"

"Promise."

Daniel asked about Mabon.

"Fake. Completely fake. Abby thought so too."

Daniel said that Mabon had convinced the people from Holyoak Hall that he believed in the whole environmental, sustainable, communal living idea, and it took years before they accepted that he was a fraud.

"But Abby and I aren't his audience," Mal said. "We're the enemy, the guardians of the status quo. He's never going to convince us, so he doesn't bother to try. He told some pretty obvious lies, like about how much time the Edwardses spent with the rest of them, but none of them contradicted him out loud."

"We can find out more if we have to." Daniel said, "There's a road block, no one's going anywhere."

Mal nodded. Then he reached his hand over to Daniel's shoulder.

"Dan, will you go to the first autopsy tomorrow? I'll do the kids ... it can't get any worse ... but I can't face it in the morning."

Daniel said, "Sure. You only have to ask."

Back upstairs, they saw PC Jones sitting next to Charlie, as Charlie looked at the police database of missing children. To Daniel's certain knowledge, PC Jones had never willingly stayed behind after the end of a shift, in his more than ten years on the job. Then he remembered the invitation to the Christening of Jones's baby girl. Dead children changed everything.

Charlie looked up. "We'll keep going, boss, but nothing so far. Most small children reported missing are child custody related."

"Well let's check that with the other residents of Gelli Terrace," Daniel said, "find out if any of them have second families."

"On it, boss," Charlie said, "and Abby said to tell you that she's made appointments for us with those solicitors first thing."

The Border Agency rang, as promised. The Edwards family had left from Tilbury, and by a miracle, only one cruise had sailed that day.

"Got them," said Daniel. The civilian researcher had left for the day, but her notes were tidy and easy to follow. It took him a few calls to reach the ship, currently somewhere in the Norwegian fjords. The person he spoke to promised to get the message through.

"Let's go home," Mal said, "they'll either ring or they won't, and we can't contact anyone else tonight."

There was a bit of light left as they set off, but it was dark by the time they got there. Mal had driven back, and all Daniel wanted was a shower and to climb into bed, wrapped around Mal. He turned the light off in the bedroom and opened the window to smell the air and listen for the owls. The sheets felt cool and crisp against his skin. He tingled with the approach of sleep, a feeling he couldn't describe, even to himself, something about the way his skin heated and almost hummed as his vision narrowed and his thoughts drifted away. Maybe he wouldn't have nightmares. He could hope. Then Mal got into bed beside him.

"You awake, Dan?"

Daniel mumbled "No."

"OK."

Mal wrapped himself round Daniel, as the big spoon, sliding his arm over Daniel's hip and fluttering his fingers over Daniel's stomach and chest. Daniel snuggled closer, feeling Mal's erection pressing into him.

"I could wake up," he said.

"I think you already did," Mal replied, stroking him gently, until Daniel turned over and kissed his boyfriend hard.

Chapter 8

He wasn't fooling himself that people would think this was the right thing to do. But it was the only thing to do. He had tried everything else.

It was a beautiful day for an autopsy. The naked, headless body lay on a stainless steel table waiting for Hector, in scrubs and apron, to reveal all its secrets. Windows set high in the walls laid stripes of sunlight across the floor and the body, reflecting off the stainless steel, a waiting scalpel catching the light and shining like a mirror. The smell of formaldehyde and decay overwhelmed Daniel as he came in from the fresh summer morning. He caught Hector's eye over the body and winced.

"Better here than when we found him," said Hector. He looked as if he hadn't slept well.

"You OK?" Daniel asked.

"Tell you after this," he said, and began to examine the body. Hector's habit was only to talk to Daniel if he had anything to show him, otherwise he dictated quietly and steadily, and reported afterwards in his office, with coffee. He had bundles of papers, reports and X-rays spread out on a table close by, and he consulted them often, peering at the body.

Daniel watched as his friend examined the dead man's limbs, then he'd re-focus and see again the way that the victim *ended* at the neck. For the first time that he could remember, he couldn't deal with what he was seeing. Hector kept a couple of chairs at the back of the autopsy suite for wobbly observers. Daniel sat in one, and closed his eyes. The sounds were grim, but better than seeing the horror again.

He heard Hector end his commentary and looked up. The mortuary assistant was making the body as decent as it could be. Daniel carefully averted his eyes and headed for Hector's office. Hector appeared a few minutes later in a set of clean scrubs, with a coffee pot in one hand and two mugs in the other.

"I think it's him," Hector said when they had their coffee, "John Edwards, I mean. The blood type matches, so does age, height and weight — as far as I can judge — and his body could be the body of a retired professional athlete. But I can't be 100% certain. We've taken fingerprints, to compare with the ones in the house, and if all else fails there's DNA, though as you know there's a bit of a wait for results."

"Did he kill himself?"

"He fired the gun. Residue on his hand and arm is clear. But that didn't mean he shot himself, only that he fired the gun. What you need to know is that he died several hours after the others. I don't know exactly when any of them died, it's never exact, but I think that the two girls and their mother died sometime in the late evening, and this man died any time between six and ten hours later."

Daniel stared at Hector, his eyes glazing over as he tried to process the information. He didn't ask if Hector was sure, because Hector wouldn't have said anything if he wasn't sure.

"Let me ring Mal," he said. By the stunned silence at the other end, Mal also had trouble working out what it meant for the investigation.

"I can't tell you any more," Hector said, "That's what the body shows, but why is down to you."

"Thanks, I think," said Daniel. They sipped their coffee. "Now tell me what's happened between you and Sasha."

"My mother is what happened. Belinda Ashleigh Lord. Lady Belinda Ashleigh Lord."

* * *

Mal looked at the photocopies, stapled together neatly at the corner.

"I made you a copy," said Jamie.

"How did you get this letter?" Mal asked.

"Ethan left it at my mother's. He must have written it before he died, just after we sailed. If I hadn't gone, maybe he'd still be here." Jamie swallowed hard, and sniffed. "Do you mind if I get a glass of water?"

Mal motioned him to stay where he was and went over to the fridge, where they kept a few bottles — filled from the tap and left to cool. He poured Jamie a glass and took it back to his office. Jamie sipped, and the tears receded.

"Sorry. I know he's been gone for over a year, but I didn't know. It's not like I could come back for the funeral. Mum didn't tell me."

"Were you and Ethan close?"

"He stayed with us when his dad kicked him out. But we were friends growing up. Same street, same school, both gay."

"But he became a sex worker and you ...?"

"Hairdresser on cruise ships. Left school, did my apprenticeship, then went off to see the world. Ethan was clever, much more than me. But my Mum is a hairdresser, she got me the apprenticeship, and encouraged me all the way. Ethan's mum is a drunk, and his dad is a drunk and a pig. He tried to stay on at school ... but I didn't know for sure what he was doing." Jamie looked down at his lap, holding his shoulders stiff, but picking at a bit of loose skin on one of his fingers, then rubbing the back of his neck as if to ease the stiffness.

"I thought it was just rich boyfriends," Jamie almost shouted, "I didn't know. Lots of boys go with rich men. It's just a bit of fun, free drinks, maybe a present. *I didn't know.*" Jamie looked at Mal, tears making his eyes shine, "*I didn't know.*"

Mal knew from the strained silence in the CID office, that people had heard Jamie. The privacy blinds were closed, so he moved round to take Jamie's hands. "How could you know? This isn't your fault Jamie. A lot of people let Ethan down, but you weren't one of them."

"*I should have known. I should have helped him.*" Jamie sobbed and pulled his hands away from Mal, making fists and banging them on the desk. "I wanted to get away, to go and cut stupid fucking hair and get a fucking tan, and I left him."

Mal took Jamie's hands again.

"Stop," he said, "stop." Jamie tried to pull his hands away, openly sobbing now, trying to hit Mal, until he fell back into his chair. Mal wrapped his arms round Jamie, holding him tightly, containing his anguish, and letting the sobs continue until the storm passed.

"I knew things weren't right," Jamie said, but he said it quietly. His face was red and swollen, his hair was wet with tears and lank from Jamie's hands, and his shirt was damp and creased.

"You didn't do this," said Mal, "and one day you'll realise that."

"I want to get those bastards. Ethan said you'd help."

"I will," said Mal.

* * *

"Sasha knows that I have to concentrate on this, she's not complaining about my not being there. But she talked to my mother on the phone by accident, and now she's terrified. I really like her, Daniel. Really like her."

Hector leaned forward over his desk, his eyes bright with worry. Daniel rubbed Hector's arm.

"Does Sasha know how you feel about her?"

Hector blushed bright red and broke into a grin.

"She should. I asked her to marry me."

"Hector! You didn't."

"I bloody did." His face fell slightly. "She sort of said yes. She's not as daft as she seems. She wants to meet my family — and she's going to hate them — and she's very determined about going to university. And then there's Arwen. Arwen has to approve."

Daniel wasn't surprised that Hector's mother had a title. He rarely spoke about his family, and Daniel had never known him to visit them, though presumably he did. His nickname, *Hooray Hector,* was meant fondly, and his colleagues teased him about being related to royalty. Hector had the confidence that came from an expensive education, but he expressed it through his work. It wasn't so much that Hector's family was a no-go area, more that Hector didn't think his background was important and everyone else took his lead.

Daniel couldn't help smiling at the thought of Hector and Sasha. They were different in every way, on the surface, but they *fitted* as a couple. "You'd leave us though," he said.

"Maybe not." Hector said, "Sasha likes it up here."

Daniel wanted to tell Hector about Jamie Maddocks. But it felt disloyal, and as if he wanted to say *hey, I've got problems too.* So he didn't. The person he needed to talk to about Jamie was Mal. He carefully didn't think about Hector moving away.

* * *

"I remembered what the scandal was," Bethan told Daniel, "John Edwards was arrested for cottaging in 2009. He wasn't charged, but it was all over the papers. Lucky for him there was another MP caught cheating on expenses the next day, so it blew over."

"Did you get the records?" Daniel asked.

Bethan gave him an *are you kidding me* look.

"You rang Glasgow police? Of course you did."

"Yep. Complaint by a member of the public. The member of the public was a serial complainer about the same offences, but someone leaked John Edwards's name to the press, who went mad. Whether an offence was actually committed wasn't clear."

"But it might have been?"

Bethan nodded.

"DCI know?"

"Not yet, I've only just put the phone down."

Daniel went into Mal's office, a bigger, tidier version of his own. Mal's office smelled of furniture polish, and another vaguely chemical smell that Daniel thought was whatever Mal used to keep his computer free of dust. Mal had a gym bag in the corner, just as Daniel did, but there was no odour of sweaty trainers or damp towels. *How does he do that?* Daniel wondered. It was one of Mal's superpowers, like the ability to keep his car clean.

"OK, the body is most likely to be John Edwards according to Hector, and he died hours after the others. Bethan has just found out that he was arrested for, but not charged, with indecent behaviour in a public place ten years ago."

"Indecent behaviour with another man?"

Daniel nodded. "Big scandal in the press, but only for a day or so."

* * *

Abby and Charlie had walked together to Jenkins and Jenkins, Solicitors and Estate Agents, and then split up. Charlie went to see the solicitor who'd made the will that had been found at *Ty Gelli*, and Abby went to talk to the estate agent who had handled the purchase of the houses. Charlie was back first, bouncing into the CID room, and then joining Mal and Daniel in Mal's office.

"I saw an actual Jenkins," he said, "I didn't know they existed. I thought it was just a name. He was only a bit older than me. Spending his time in an office making wills, poor bloke." He looked at Mal and Daniel and decided to change tack, producing his notebook. "So, anyway, both John and Hayley Edwards went to the first appointment, and both returned to sign the wills a week later. They made *Mirror Wills* basically leaving everything to each other, and then to their children. They were new wills because they'd moved back from the USA and they weren't sure if the law was different."

The date on the wills found in the house, and at the solicitor was the same.

"What happens to the money now?" Daniel asked.

"It looks like it goes to the little boy, if he is their son, or John's sister if he isn't. The only children mentioned are the two girls, but Dafydd wouldn't have been born by then."

"Did they say who would look after the children if they died?" Daniel asked. There had been long discussions about guardianship of his nephew and niece, and it had been included in his sister's and brother-in-law's will.

"John's sister," Charlie said.

Daniel thought that it was odd that they hadn't gone back to include Dafydd, or to set up some kind of trust for the children. It was unusual to have such simple arrangements if the information about the family's wealth was correct. He would have expected something more complicated and *tax efficient* than a small town solicitor's efforts. He said as much.

"Mr Jenkins said the same. He was surprised that we hadn't found more up to date wills. *A placeholder will* is what he called it. But he said that it wasn't tax planning or trust funds that he thought was next on the list. He thought it would be divorce."

Both Daniel and Mal sat up. If John Edwards had killed his family, a threat of divorce was a likely cause. Except that the will had been made three years before, and they had found no signs of divorce papers.

"They weren't arguing or anything obvious," Charlie continued, "but Jenkins says he's done lots of divorces and he got the vibe. The only other thing, is that John Edwards went back about three months ago. He wanted to talk about giving the houses in Gelli Terrace to their tenants, but he never followed it up."

"*Giving*, not selling?"

"Giving," Charlie confirmed.

* * *

Abby stepped over the threshold of the estate agent part of Jenkins and Jenkins, and into the past. Wood panelling dominated the decor, complemented by green leather chairs with brass rivets. The inside of the shop was dark after the bright sunshine outside, the windows

71

obscured by advertisements for properties for sale and to rent. Two dark wood desks were set well back from the street door, and it took a moment for Abby's eyes to adjust. She heard the *can I help you?* before being able to make out a figure behind one of the desks. She crossed the brown Linoleum and found herself face to face with a familiar-looking woman, dressed in a dark blouse and pearls, with meticulously waved hair, so well lacquered that it moved as a single piece.

"Abby Price, is it?" the woman said, and Abby remembered who she was — the mother of one of her school friends. She'd been round to this woman's house for her tea more than once.

"Hi, Mrs Jones," she said, and showed her warrant card, "I've come to talk about the houses in Gelli."

"Of course you have, lovely. Coffee?"

As Magda (as Mrs Jones insisted on being called) made coffee for them both, they got themselves caught up on her friend Emily's doings, and Abby said how much she was enjoying her job, and that her family was well, thank you.

"That's a terrible thing, that happened in Gelli," Magda said, "I remember showing them the house, them and the two little girls. The girls sounded like Americans. And now they're all dead?"

Abby gave the stock explanation of *ongoing investigation, awaiting formal identification, sorry can't discuss it.* She made a mental note to be very careful about how she phrased her questions because Magda was a perfect demonstration of the speed at which gossip circulates in a small town.

"What can you tell me about *Ty Gelli*?" she began.

"It was lovely. Old couple had it for ever, then he died and she went into a home and their son came and had it all done up. They took it down to the bare bricks they did, but they replaced everything with top quality work — which isn't always the case, as I'm sure you know." Magda looked pointedly in the direction of the now-closed North Wales

Estates, a modern estate agency used until a few months before as a front for property fraud. Abby nodded.

"You did know that all the cottages were for sale too? With tenants?" Abby nodded again.

"Not the usual package, but they could have bought the house on its own. They had plenty of money — he was a famous footballer — which was probably good because those cottages don't bring in much rent ... *anyway* what did you want to know?"

"I was hoping for a list of tenants, and to know if they were all there when the Edwardses bought the house."

Magda leaned forward, as if to speak confidentially, even though there was no one else in the shop.

"See, I'm not a licensed conveyancer, so one of the solicitors has to sign off on it all, but just between us, I do most of the paperwork. I remember the Gelli houses because it was a bit different. We let the cottages from this office, and collect the rent and so on, and those Edwardses, they didn't want the renters to know that they'd bought the cottages. Thought it would be awkward, finding out that your new neighbour is also your landlord, if you get me?"

Abby did get it.

"So Mr Jenkins, young Rhys that is, he set up a company for them — Gelli Homes — and that's who owns the cottages as far as the tenants know."

Abby asked if Jenkins and Jenkins were still the managers, collecting the rent and finding new tenants. Magda nodded vigorously, her helmet of hair banging against her forehead.

"Oh yes, nothings changed. It's just that no one knew who the new owner was."

If you knew, thought Abby, half the town would know. But probably not the people she had met yesterday in Gelli. She asked for a list of tenants. Magda stood up and moved to a row of filing cabinets. The tenants were James Protheroe, Mabon and his friends and a Jack Wall in the last house. Only Wall and Protheroe pre-dated the Edwardses.

"I'll make you copies," she said.

"I was in Gelli yesterday," said Abby, "and the middle houses had all been knocked into one downstairs. Did the Edwardses agree to that?"

"Oh yes. It was an odd thing to want to do, but John Edwards seemed to think highly of that ap Richardson and his friends. He came and saw Mr Jenkins, young Rhys, John Edwards that is, and he said he didn't mind. He could always put it back together again he said. He won't now though, will he?"

Chapter 9

F riends turned out not to be friends. Everyone wanted a piece of him, but no one ever gave anything back.

Mal had thought of PC Jones as a time server, if he thought about him at all. But something about this case seemed to have woken him up. As they parked outside *Ty Gelli*, Jones said "The orange camper has gone, sir." Mal remembered the camper van as another symbol of hippiedom, and Jones was right — it was missing.

"Gone shopping maybe? Radio the road block and ask when it went."

Mal heard the answer. No orange camper had passed the road block in either direction. No vehicles had passed from Gelli towards town. The only vehicles to have passed from town to Gelli were the CSIs and now PC Jones and Mal. A couple of journalists had been turned away.

"Have a look round," said Mal, "they might have moved it. Check along the road to the farm." PC Jones nodded and said he'd ring if he found the camper.

Mal got out of the car and asked the PC with the clipboard if he would fetch Paul Jarvis.

"Nothing much new," Jarvis said, when he appeared in his paper suit, with his mask dangling from one ear. "We're having a look at the bedrooms. Someone's been sleeping in the spare bed, though how recently I can't tell. There's men's and women's stuff in the main bedroom."

Mal thanked him, and went to call on the commune.

Mel Ward answered the door. Over her shoulder Mal saw that the table was being used for the children to do their schoolwork, with help from two of the adults. Of the other adults there was no sign.

"I have a couple more questions," he said, "it shouldn't take long."

"Sure, happy to help," Mel said, but he noticed that she wiped her hands down her skirt, as if she was nervous. One of the children dropped something on the floor, and Mel flinched.

"Is something wrong?" he asked.

"No! Why would anything be wrong?" Her voice had risen, was almost shrill.

Mal's phone rang. "Excuse me," he said and stepped back outside to take the call.

"The orange camper isn't here, sir. I'm at the farm now, and I've been as far up the track as I can get. No camper."

Mal thanked him and went back into the house.

"Who took the orange camper van?" he asked Mel, who had been joined by Cai.

"Mabon," said Cai, "he's had to go back to his old place. They needed his help."

Cai gave off a hint of body odour, and he kept looking over at the children's table, as if expecting Mabon to jump out from behind it. Mel had started biting the skin at the end of her fingers.

"I thought we'd made it clear that you all needed to stay local for the time being," Mal said.

"Can you do that?" Cai asked, "Make us stay here, even though we've done nothing wrong? Because this isn't a good place right now. We aren't even being told what's happened."

"I need the registration number of the camper van." Mal said, "and

76

the names of the other people who have gone with Mabon. The two older boys is it?" Mel gasped, and wrapped her arms round herself.

Cai shook his head. "No, just Mabon," he said.

"Don't the boys do schoolwork?" Mal asked, "Please don't lie to me. There were two boys here yesterday, and there is no sign of either of them today."

"They'll all be back soon," Mel said, with a confidence, that Mal didn't believe.

"I hope so," said Mal, "in the meantime, I want the registration of the van, and the names of the boys."

All he managed to get was a guess at the registration number, and that Mabon had taken the boys, Ben and Josh, to his "old place", Holyoak Hall, in Devon. From what Daniel had said, it wasn't likely that anyone from Holyoak Hall had asked Mabon to visit. The tension in the room generated by Cai and Mel began to affect the children. One of the young ones began to cry, and another started banging things on the table.

Mal ignored them, along with the increasing agitation of the adults. "What do you know about Mr Wall, who lives in the last house?" he asked.

"He's gone travelling," said Cai, "won't be back for months yet."

The tension in the room decreased a little.

"I *know* that Mabon hasn't gone to Devon," he said.

The tension in the air ratcheted up again. Mal saw that Mel was chewing her fingers, and remembered that one of the boys was hers.

"Josh is your son, Mel?" he asked, "Is he Mabon's son too?"

"Not biologically," Mel replied, "but he parents equally."

Whatever that means, thought Mal.

Cai stepped closer to Mal, getting into his personal space.

"What's it got to do with you, who's kid is whose?" he spat at Mal. Cai raised his hand as if to push Mal back towards the door.

"Don't," Mal said quietly.

One of Mel's little girls, Pixie, Mal thought, crept away from the table and threw her arm around her mother's legs, sucking the thumb on her other hand. The other girl grasped her sister's hand and pulled the thumb out of her mouth. "Mum, when's Josh coming back, Mum? Mum."

Cai put his hand up again, the bracelets on his arm catching the sunlight. Becca said "Cai, no." Her voice was shaking. Everyone else in the room was frozen. Mel's daughter had shrunk against her sister and stopped trying to get Mel's attention. Mal couldn't let the children see any more of this. He beckoned Cai, and stepped into the sun-drenched road. A moment later Mel and Becca followed, closing the door behind themselves.

"This is nothing to do with you," Cai said, his voice tight and high-pitched.

"Listen," said Mal, "four people were killed the night before last. Everyone denies hearing or seeing anything, and at least some of you are lying about it. Mabon has disappeared with two of your children, and you're lying about that too. I think everything you've told me is lies. I think you're terrified for the safety of those children. The quickest way you can get them back is to tell me the truth."

"You're talking crap, pig," said Cai, but the tremble in his body betrayed him. "We're telling you *nothing.*"

Chapter 10

He thought that his children loved him unconditionally. He was wrong. They conspired with the others.

"I think they're frightened," Mal told Daniel, and after hearing him out, Daniel agreed.

"Mabon has taken those two boys hostage," said Mal, "and we have to find them before anyone in the commune will tell us the truth. I can believe that old James Protheroe didn't hear those shots, but not that no one heard them."

They were back on the smokers' bench in the sun, both with coffee. Mal was about to head over to Wrexham for the other autopsies, and not looking forward to it.

Daniel squeezed Mal's hand.

"Even Hector is going to struggle with autopsies on the children," he said.

Daniel took the call from John Edwards senior, ringing from somewhere afloat on the Norwegian fjords. There was no easy way to break the news, and he could hear the cries of grief from John's mother and sister, and the crack in John senior's voice. He had to say that they thought that the bodies were those of John, Hayley and the girls, but that they didn't yet know what had happened.

"So you don't *know* it's them?" John asked, with no real hope in his voice. There was a clatter. "I'm sorry, the phone slipped from my hand." Daniel heard a woman's voice say *"Tell him we'll come straight back."*

"We need to make arrangements, Inspector, perhaps I could call you later?"

"Of course," said Daniel, "but there is one question I need to ask. Did John and Hayley have a little boy? Dafydd? About eighteen months old?"

"What?"

Daniel repeated his question.

"No. Two girls, Seren and Stella. I'm sorry, I don't understand."

Nor do I, thought Daniel, *nor do I.*

How hard can it be to find an orange camper van? Mal had spent a few minutes updating Charlie about the van before he had to leave for Wrexham and the autopsy suite. Even with a partial registration, Charlie found the van on the DVLA database.

"Leave it to me, boss," said Charlie, "he won't have got far. Those things don't go very fast."

But by the time Mal left, Charlie had found no sign of the van.

"He's keeping to the back roads," said Charlie.

"Or he's dumped the van," said Mal, "so get the word out to anywhere you can think of that it might have been left."

* * *

Daniel wanted to see the baby. That was the top and bottom of it. He could have told Veronica on the phone that little Dafydd might not be John and Hayley Edwards's son, but he wanted to see the baby. On the way, he'd stopped at the best of the gift shops and bought a teddy bear suitable for a child of Dafydd's age, and it was in a brightly coloured bag under his arm.

Veronica let him in to the unassuming terraced house and led him to the kitchen at the back. There was an extension into the garden, with a sofa and toys. On the sofa a middle-aged woman was playing with Dafydd. They both looked up as Daniel and Veronica came into the room. Dafydd's face lit up into a huge smile and he held his arms out. Daniel put his parcel down and after a nod from Veronica, swung the little boy up, making him laugh.

"Hi, Dafydd," said Daniel, loving the weight of the child, his warmth and solidity.

"Man," said Dafydd, "man."

"I brought you a present," said Daniel, and then said it again in Welsh. "Would you like a present Dafydd?"

"Yep," he answered.

"Sit down," said the middle-aged woman, indicating the sofa. Veronica introduced her as Mary Kelly.

"Mary is our emergency baby person," said Veronica, and Daniel had to tell her that the emergency wouldn't be coming to an end straight away.

"All we know so far is who he probably isn't," he said, "John Edwards's father says that he isn't his son's child, and we've already started looking at reports of missing children fitting his description."

He let the two women process the information, while he helped Dafydd open his present.

"Beh," he said, and kissed the teddy.

"Your bear, Dafydd," said Daniel, "It's safe for his age," he said to

81

Veronica, who had already seen the label. She smiled to herself, loving the thought of Daniel knowing about age-appropriate teddy bears.

Mary said, "Well he didn't appear by magic, someone must know who he is."

"We'll find his parents," said Daniel, with more confidence than he felt. Dafydd presented him with the teddy. Daniel kissed it and gave it back. "Dafydd's bear, he's for you, *cariad,* what are you going to call him?"

"Beh," was the answer.

"We've got reports of children his age being abducted by parents in custody cases," Daniel said, and Veronica scowled. "We're going to check every one that might be him, and if we have to, we'll go to the press."

"But Gelli is in the middle of nowhere. You found him in the early morning. He *must* have come from one of those houses."

Either that, or he'd been abandoned, by someone who'd driven away before he and Mal had arrived. But he didn't believe that, any more than he believed in the tooth fairy. The people in the cottages had told them that Dafydd belonged to Hayley and John. John's parents said he didn't. Someone was lying.

"I wouldn't have let you go," he said to Dafydd, who was having fun pulling on Daniel's tie.

"Yep," said Dafydd.

"Have you thought of applying to be a foster carer," said Mary Kelly, "they're always short of people, and you're good with him."

"I'm not sure it's compatible with police work," Daniel said.

"Police work isn't mandatory," said Veronica.

"It is if you want to pay the mortgage, and sadly I have to get back to it."

He stood up, giving the baby one last cuddle. "I've got to go back to work now, Dafydd. I've got to find your mam and dad."

82

He gave the little boy back to Mary.

"Bye bye, Dafydd," he said.

"Bye," said Dafydd with a little wave.

Veronica walked him to the door.

"Who could do that?" Daniel asked, "abandon a child? What if we hadn't come along?"

Veronica put her hand on his arm. "People do terrible things when they're under stress, or frightened. Things they didn't mean to do, or things that seemed right at the time. You'll find them."

Damn right I will.

* * *

Hector had tried to tell Sasha.

"My family are awful. Really awful. You'll hate them."

But Sasha had insisted that if Hector was serious about getting married, she wanted to meet them.

"I'm this rough tart with a kid, from the Welsh Valleys. They'll take one look at me and you'll be cut off without a penny."

"I wasn't getting anything anyway," he said.

Hector thought of the "family home" — a cold and comfortless pile in the Hertfordshire countryside, in need of endless and expensive repairs — and thanked the universe for the nth time, that as an unexpected third son, its upkeep was nothing to do with him. He'd met Sasha's family at her sister's wedding, and Sasha had reported that they thought he was OK. "Which is pretty good, considering you're English," she'd said.

He didn't care what his family thought about Sasha. They didn't approve of his choice to move to rural north Wales, or his choice of pathology as his specialism. But then, he didn't approve of their support for the local hunt, their snobbery about having a title, or their sending small children away to boarding school. He didn't dislike them, and he didn't think they disliked him. His brothers had looked out for him at school. His father had found a friend, who knew someone, who made sure that he got an interview for medical school. He was sure that they would come to his wedding, and he supposed they'd be sorry if anything bad happened to him. He looked up at Mal, who was watching him work, and whose family pretended he didn't exist, and thought that maybe his own family weren't so bad, for all their snobbery.

"Go and sit down," he told his friend, "I don't want you to watch. If there's anything you need to see, I'll call you."

He had completed the autopsy on Hayley Edwards, and there was no longer any reason to delay the examination of the two girls.

Mal shook his head, but when Hector and the mortuary assistant lifted the body of the older girl onto the table, Mal went pale and went to sit down, and looked hard at the floor.

Hector had expected to find that the girls had been smothered, and he did.

"There's no sign that either of them struggled, so I think we can assume that they were drugged," he told Mal. He sent samples to be tested for sleeping tablets. Mal made a note to check whether John or Hayley had been prescribed anything that could have been used.

"They didn't know," Hector said, "I'm certain of it."

"I'm not sure that makes it any better," said Mal.

"No. I don't think it does."

* * *

84

The road back from Wrexham was busy with commuters on their way home from work, slowing the traffic enough that Mal could think as well as drive. He didn't like his thoughts. The case was bad enough, but he had to tell Daniel about Jamie's story and he didn't expect it to go well. Daniel had grown up in a family where people liked him. They might not have been over the moon that he was gay, but they still liked him. Mal knew that Daniel had faced his fair share of homophobia in school, and in the police, but he didn't know what it was to have his family turn against him, to be told in ways subtle and not so subtle, that he was less valuable than his siblings.

Mal had tried to keep his sexuality hidden, but in a small house with a lot of people, things got noticed. His brothers talked about girls and rugby and thought a good night out was getting smashed in Ponty. He went to the gym instead. He couldn't remember not knowing that he was gay. He liked girls, but not in the way that his brothers liked them. At the gym, he looked at the men, and every so often, one of them looked back at him, until he got spotted by a friend of his father's and the pretence was over. He stuck it out at home by keeping as far from his father and his father's fists as he could. His mother made sure that he had food, but that was as far as she was prepared to stand up to her husband. She didn't want him to leave, but he wasn't part of the family any more. So he went to school, spent as long as he could in the library, and the gym, and got his brother Huw to let him into the bedroom window when he came home, so that his dad wouldn't know he was in the house.

He took a day off school to go for an interview with the Metropolitan Police. A month later a letter with the Met's logo arrived. Mal's father opened it, assuming, as he always did, that Mal was in trouble. When he saw that it was a job offer, the explosion could have been heard in Cardiff. Mal grabbed the letter and ran, and never went back. He wasn't homeless for long, but it was long enough. He'd told Daniel that his

85

father didn't speak to him because he'd joined the London police. He hadn't told Daniel about the violence, or the homophobia, and he didn't want to. But he understood, at a visceral level, why Ethan had killed himself, and he couldn't do nothing.

That first night after he ran away from home, he went to his oldest sister and her brand new husband in Cardiff.

"You can't stay here, Maldi, Dad's been on the phone." He'd cried then, as he understood the magnitude of what had happened.

"Huw said he'd bring my things here in the morning," he said.

"One night," she'd said, "but that's all." He could see her lips tighten, arms crossed over her chest, everything about her rejecting the brother she'd grown up with. She'd helped their mother feed and wash him as a baby, walked with him to school and now she wanted nothing to do with him.

Huw brought a backpack full of Mal's things, and as much money as he had been able to get together. It wasn't going to be enough to keep him for the month before he had to report to the police college in Hendon. They sat on the wall outside his sister's house, both in shock.

"This job, Huw, it's what I want," Mal found himself comforting his brother, "I'd have been gone in a month anyway."

"Dad's just *wrong*," said Huw, "everyone knows it, no one does anything."

Mal told Huw to go home and not make any waves. They'd walked down to the bus station together, and it had been twenty years until he saw any of them again. Ethan had brought it all back — the fear, the filthy squat, the battle to keep clean, the men who offered a bed for the night, counting the days until he could report for work, the constant low level anxiety and the spikes of pure terror. Above all, he remembered the numbness of being cut off from everything that was familiar, the longing to see a known face, hear a voice from home, and knowing that he wouldn't, that he wasn't wanted and that there was no way back.

* * *

"We've found the van, sir," said Charlie, as Mal walked into the CID room, "trouble is, there's no one in it." A map on Charlie's computer screen showed a marker where two major roads crossed, about twenty miles south of Melin Tywyll.

"It's on every bus route, and he could get to the train from Ruabon from the bus. Or someone could have picked him up."

"You're trying the bus companies?"

"Yes, sir, nothing yet."

Mal looked at the map. The two major roads took the only possible route through the mountainous terrain. To the south were the Berwyn mountains, a huge, wild area, with few people. It would be easy to hide in the mountains, as long as you had food and the weather stayed kind. He crossed his fingers that Mabon had caught a bus, and that he and the two boys were on their way to somewhere the police could pick them up. But when the phone rang, it was to report that no one matching Mabon's description had caught a bus in any direction since Mabon had disappeared.

"Have we got someone down there, checking the van?" Mal asked Charlie, who nodded.

"It's locked up, and there aren't any houses nearby."

"We'd better keep an eye on it." Mal needed to ask Sophie for yet another uniformed officer to keep watch, on top of the officers running the roadblock to Gelli. He thought he'd better take some decent coffee as a peace offering.

Chapter 11

He remembered the funeral of a teammate who had killed himself. The preacher stood over the grave and said no amount of money would have saved him.

Daniel's hands shook on the coffee mug as he stared at his sister across her kitchen table. Dave and the twins were out somewhere, and Megan had asked Daniel to call in on his way home. He put the mug down as carefully as he could and stood up. The chair tilted, and almost fell, but he caught it just in time. He walked very carefully to the back door, instructing his feet and legs to do what they should have done automatically. He opened the door to leave.

"Wait, Dan, wait."

"I'm OK," he said, though she hadn't asked, "I have to go back to work."

He carried on instructing his feet to move, although he kept misjudging the distance between foot and pavement, and foot and stairs, until he reached his office on the top floor of the police station. Once there, he carefully closed the door and the blinds, sat down and laid his head in his arms on the desk, and let the tears fall.

It was up to Megan and Dave where they lived. It was up to Hector whether he needed to move away to be with Sasha. None of them owed him anything. He could visit. He could talk to them on the phone. He had Mal. Sorrow washed over him in waves. As he lost control, his mind took him back under the stage in the Burns and Wood Building, knowing that the only way out was to hurt Andy Carter as badly as he could. He'd done it, and then Andy Carter was killed. He heard the gunfire, over and over again, smelled the blood, saw the body collapse onto the dirty floor. The failure was his. The moment he should have acted, and didn't. Because of his failure, Mal had been shot. He couldn't get past it.

Another wave of sorrow. Baby Dafydd with no family to care for him. The little body that he had held against his bare flesh had no one. The cries for his mam, who wasn't coming.

He hid his face in his arms and he cried for all of them, and for himself. Because his sister and her family were going to move to Spain, and it was one more loss. They had been making plans for months and kept them secret. It felt like a betrayal of everything he'd believed about his sister. His friend was hoping to get married and to start a new life, and what should have made him happy, made him sad, and how pathetic and selfish was that?

After an hour, or maybe two, he went home.

Mal was waiting for him with a beer and a big plate of salad, lots of it home-grown. He'd set a table up in front of the house, where they could look out over the valley. Two chairs were next to one another. Daniel took the beer and drank, but looked blankly at the food.

"What did Megan want?" Mal asked.

Daniel shook his head.

"Something's wrong, I'm not daft."

Daniel shook his head again and drank more beer. "I'm fine."

"Dan, you're not fine. Tell me what's happened."

Daniel told himself to relax, to look at his boyfriend, not to stare at his beer bottle.

89

"Just the case. What did Jamie Maddocks want?"

"To say that Ethan left him a letter, naming two other young prostitutes who killed themselves after being assaulted by the police."

Daniel put his beer down on the table.

"Don't make this your problem, Maldwyn."

"It's already my problem. No one else wants to know."

"No, Mal, just no. Those people put you in hospital once. You can't do this." Daniel heard his voice rising, the note of panic. Mal's face was set in stubborn lines.

"You've already said yes, haven't you? Were you going to tell me? Or just disappear?" He knew that he was being unfair, but he couldn't stop. What right had Mal to put himself in the line of fire, again?

"I'm never going to disappear, unless you tell me to," Mal said.

Daniel wanted to tell Mal about Megan, his twin, the person he thought he knew best in the world. About how she had been planning to leave Wales for Spain — only for a year, Dan, only for a year — and she hadn't told him, until it was all fixed. But he couldn't speak. The words froze in his mouth. He saw Andy Carter, and the road in Gelli, through the eyes of a child, an abandoned child, the world bright and unfamiliar, needing his mother or his father, to help him make sense of it all. The sorrow slammed into him again.

"Everyone wants to leave," said Daniel, and Mal saw the pain in his eyes. Daniel got up and went into the house. Mal heard the bedroom door close. He picked up the dinner things and put them in the kitchen. He moved slowly, deliberately, putting the forks into the dishwasher, washing the salad bowl, cleaning the surfaces, dragging out jobs that should take seconds, because he was afraid to go upstairs. In the end there was no choice. Daniel was lying on his front, head in the pillow, unmoving. His clothes were in a heap on the floor.

"You OK?" he said, picking up Daniel's things and beginning to fold them over a chair.

"Just get into bed."

"I'm not going to leave you."

"Good." Daniel turned his back on Mal.

Mal thought he wouldn't sleep, but he must have done, because he woke to feel Daniel pressed against him, though still facing away. Mal pressed his lips to the curve between Daniel's neck and his shoulder, feeling Daniel's pulse, and breathing in the familiar scent of him, sweaty from sleep. He pressed his chest against Daniel's back, hard muscle against hard muscle. His nipples lit up, and his hand moved over Daniel's ribs, down to his hard stomach and even harder cock. Daniel didn't move or speak.

Mal stroked Daniel's nipples, feeling them harden, and hearing a tiny moan. Mal felt his cock twitch in response, and Daniel felt warmer against his skin. He pushed the covers back, so the breezes from the open window raised the hairs on their bodies, as they brought the sounds of the night, and the scent of the wisteria into the room with them. "I love you, Daniel Owen," Mal whispered, and kissed his neck again. The only response was a sigh.

Mal caressed Daniel's neck with his tongue, running it gently up to Daniel's ear in a way that he knew Daniel loved. He felt Daniel's shiver of pleasure and it made him happy. He did it again, and again, and played with Daniel's nipples, listening to the little moans. He slid an arm underneath Daniel and pulled him closer, pinning Daniel's arms to his side, and then he moved his other hand to stroke Daniel's cock, teasing him, touching him, and stopping whenever Daniel tried to thrust against his hand. Daniel wriggled, but Mal held him tighter, nibbling Daniel's earlobe, and wrapping his hand around Daniel's cock and slowly, slowly starting to move it up and down.

"Maldwyn, stop."

Mal stopped moving his hand. He rolled onto his back, and propped himself against the pillows, still holding Daniel captive.

"Stop torturing me. Don't stop."

"Stop. Don't stop. What shall I do?"

In answer, Daniel thrust against Mal's hand. Mal felt his own erection against Daniel's arse, and Daniel felt it too and opened his legs with a moan. Mal wrapped his hand around Daniel's cock again and resumed the torture, stopping whenever he felt Daniel getting close, until Daniel was whimpering.

"Are you in pain, love? Shall I stop?"

"Don't you fucking dare."

Mal stopped. "I want to kiss you," he said, and moved so that Daniel could turn to him. He took Daniel's face in his hands and their two bodies came together. All Mal's senses ignited. He felt Daniel's hands on his body, their skin touching, tongues and lips moving together. Both their cocks were leaking, and Mal reached down to hold them both. Daniel had the same thought and their hands met, wrapping themselves together until Mal didn't know where he ended and Daniel began. He felt Daniel's body clench and Daniel cried out. Then his own orgasm hit and he forgot everything.

*

"We agreed to talk about things. And we're not."

"Talk then," said Mal, refilling his mug from the coffee pot.

"That's the last of the coffee."

"I'll make more, now talk."

Daniel watched as Mal put water in the kettle, rinsed out the coffee pot and added fresh coffee. He wanted to tell Mal about Megan, and about his misery over the little boy, the feelings of sorrow that overwhelmed him without warning, the images of Andy Carter that he couldn't get rid of. Instead he said,

"I was serious about Jamie Maddocks. You can't go up against those guys again. You don't work there any more and no one will help you."

"Two other boys, Daniel. Dead because of what the police did. We can't just pretend it didn't happen."

"Then don't go by yourself. Wait until this case is over and we'll do it together."

"I promised Jamie I'd help, and I will. But that's not all that's wrong with you, is it?"

Daniel turned his head away, Mal hadn't reacted to his offer of help with Jamie. He didn't want to talk about Megan, or about the little boy, or about Andy Carter. So he moved back onto the safer ground of the case.

"Those hippies. They let me think the baby was John and Hayley's. You've talked to them about everything else but not that. I want to go back and ask them."

"Okay, we'll go and ask them together."

* * *

Gelli was showing signs of everything that had happened over the last couple of days. There were a few paper coffee cups abandoned beside the road. Daniel picked them up one at a time and took them back to the car. Police tape barred entry to the path beside the Edwards's house and lined the route to the back door. It had only been two days but already the tape was looking dusty from the passage of feet and vehicles on the dry road. Outside the hippies' house the flowers were starting to wilt. No one had remembered to water them.

In the distance Daniel could hear the sounds of chainsaws, clear-felling in a nearby valley. Over that, birdsong. Blackbirds, robins,

93

corvids, all arguing about territory, stealing each other's nesting materials, trying to ensure their families were fed. Outside, the overwhelming smell was of spring greenery. A door opened, and James Protheroe called them in. Inside, things were not so sweet. Mal introduced Daniel, who was trying not to breathe through his nose, or to touch any of the greasy, cat hair covered furniture. The fire remained unlit, but the smell was still strong, overlaid this morning with the odour of fried eggs and burned toast. Protheroe smirked and mumbled something about liking to see Daniel did have proper clothes.

"I thought you'd be back to talk to me some more," he said, "You've been to talk to those hippies. You don't want to trust a word any of them says."

"I was planning on talking to you today," said Mal, "I wanted to ask if you'd seen the orange camper van drive off yesterday. Probably in the late afternoon or early evening."

"More likely the middle of the night," Protheroe grumbled, "They're always carrying on late at night."

"Is that when Mabon went?" Mal asked, knowing that the road block had been in place and that Mabon hadn't passed it.

"Maybe. It's usually when they get up to stuff. Coming and going. Lights."

"What stuff?" Mal asked, putting a harder edge into his voice. He felt sorry for Protheroe, but wary that the old man was trying to cause trouble where none was needed. He hadn't heard the shots, so how did he know what went on late at night?

Protheroe sighed and sat down in the chair nearest to the fire. It had a grease stain at his head height, and the arms had frayed seams.

"Not so much now," he said, "but when that fella was in the end house ..." He deflated in front of them, his energy departing with each sigh. "He was a nice fella, Jack. The only one who came to talk to me. The others say hello, but they don't want to talk, not even the footballer, but that Jack, he could have a proper conversation."

"What was he like?"

"Bit of a pansy, as we used to say in the army. Wrote books. Grew flowers and not all these vegetables."

"What kinds of books?"

"No idea." Protheroe waved his arm around the living room, which was bereft of any reading matter at all.

"He built that shed-thing in his garden, said it was his *retreat.* I told him that he didn't know the meaning of the word, but he just laughed." Protheroe shook his head, and looked down. "Nice bloke." Mal renewed his resolution to find out if there was any help out there for the old man. He'd made notes to contact the Welsh Guards, but he needed to actually do it.

"So all these night time movements stopped when Mr Wall went travelling?" Mal asked.

"About then. I don't know where he went though. He didn't say anything about going, just disappeared, like."

"And the comings and goings, who was involved?"

"All of them. The footballers and the hippies. I didn't keep a list."

"Mr Protheroe," said Daniel, "do you remember when we first met, I had a little boy? We found him in the middle of the road. That's why we stopped."

Protheroe nodded, with a sly smile, "Not likely to forget, am I?"

"The people in the other houses said the little boy was called Dafydd, and that he was the Edwards's child. Is that what you thought?"

"Is what what I thought?"

"Who did you think that child belonged to?"

Protheroe tilted his head to one side, like a puzzled bird, and he looked at nothing, before shaking his head and saying that he didn't know.

"I don't think he was always here though. But I couldn't tell you when he came."

Happy to be away from the smelly oppression of Protheroe's house, Mal and Daniel leaned against Mal's car, facing the gardens and the hills on the far side of the river, and drank coffee from their flask. The sound of the chainsaws stopped suddenly, and the birdsong seemed louder in the silence. Mal reached for Daniel's hand, twining their fingers together, feeling Daniel stroking the hairs on the back of his hand. There were arguments to come, he knew, about Jamie Maddocks, and whatever it was that Daniel wasn't telling him, but for now, this was enough. He put his coffee down on the ground, took Daniel's from his hand and put it down too. Then he pulled Daniel towards him and kissed him. Daniel tasted of coffee, and himself.

Chapter 12

N o amount of money, nothing from this world could protect him. The more he tried to help, the more the sharks wanted from him.

Cai stood sideways on to the open door, his arms folded, his eyes looking anywhere but at Daniel and Mal.

"I thought we'd made ourselves clear. We've got nothing to say to you."

Mal kept back, in the hope that Daniel would have more luck.

"Believe it or not, we're trying to help," said Daniel, "We need to find the little boy's parents, and your own sons. We've found the orange camper van, but not the boys."

Cai looked at Daniel and then looked away.

"The boys are with Mabon."

"The problem is that we don't know where Mabon has taken them." Daniel kept his voice soft.

"He'll bring them back."

"I'm sure he will. But when? We have questions for him, and we want to make sure that the boys are safe."

"He'll come back when you lot leave us alone."

And that was it, Daniel thought, Mabon was holding the boys hostage until the police gave up and went away. Only it wasn't going to work.

Because there were secrets here and one way or another they were going to be told.

Mal said, "If you don't want to talk to us here, you can talk to us in a formal interview, under caution, at the police station. All of you. Separately. Your choice."

Cai slipped back inside the house and shut the door. They heard the lock turn.

"That went well," Daniel said.

"Wait and see," Mal replied.

Raised voices came from inside the house, and the sound of a baby crying. Another sound, like a chair being knocked over, then a high pitched woman's voice. "I'm going to talk to them. Our friends are *dead* ..." Then they heard a man's angry voice and the unmistakable sound of a slap, followed by a cry of pain.

Mal began to hammer on the door as Daniel belted round the end of the terrace to the back door. Which stood open. He stepped inside.

"Please let my colleague in," he said, "this has gone on long enough."

Mel, Cai and Bethany looked at him. Bethany had a red mark on her face, and a baby in her arms. Of Tom and Becca and the rest of the children, there was no sign. Cai opened the front door.

"I'm so sorry Beth," said Mel, "I don't know what came over me,"

"Let's all sit down and have a cup of tèa," said Daniel.

"A cup of tea?" Bethany's voice hovered on the edge of hysteria, "A cup of tea will make everything alright?" Mel guided her to one of the sofas, and sat down next to her, wrapping her arms around both Bethany and the baby, who grizzled into her mother's shoulder.

Daniel saw Mal filling a kettle and taking mugs down from hooks above the work surface. Tea bags were in a clearly labelled tin.

"Not orange tea, please, Maldwyn,"

Mal sniffed at the tea bags and pulled a face. "It's herb tea."

"Now you're complaining about the fucking tea?" Cai had begun to pace between the front door and the kitchen, clenching and releasing his hands.

"Please come and sit down, sir," said Daniel, leading the way.

Cai resisted, but sat down when Daniel smiled and patted the sofa. Bethany's sobs had begun to ease, helping the emotional temperature to drop.

"We're curious about your other neighbour, Jack Wall," said Daniel, "I know that he's away, but it would be good if we could contact him. Any ideas?"

He could see from Cai's face that his instinct was to deny all knowledge of Wall's whereabouts, so he turned to Mel.

"No idea. He had been talking about going away for months and then one day he went."

"Didn't you see him go?"

Mel shook her head as Cai said "Sure we did Mel. Taxi came. Manchester airport. Greece maybe?"

Mel looked puzzled. "I must have been out."

Daniel asked Bethany if he knew where Wall had gone, but she shrugged.

Mal brought the tea and gave everyone a cup. He asked if anyone could recall exactly when Jack Wall had left. No one could. Sometime in the winter was the vague consensus.

"Last thing," said Daniel, "you remember that DCI Kent and I stopped here because we found a child in the road in front of your houses?"

They all looked at him, but didn't acknowledge the question.

"Mel, you called the baby *Dafydd*, and more than one of you told DCI Kent that he was one of John and Hayley's children."

"We may have done, so what?" Cai countered.

"Would you be surprised to learn that John's father denies all knowledge of a third child?"

99

"I think I can hear Becca and Tom with the children," said Mel, scrambling to her feet, sloshing her tea onto the floor. "Yes, it's them. Could you come back another time? Because it upsets the younger children ... this whole police thing. I'm sorry."

Cai went to the front door and held it open.

"I'm sorry too," Daniel said to him, "because until we find out what happened here, we're going to keep coming back."

"What aren't they telling lies about?" Daniel asked. They walked up the road towards the farm, the same road that they'd run down three days before.

"We probably are upsetting the children," said Mal, "That might be true."

"They're lying because Mabon has taken those two boys hostage. Everything about the three of them says they're scared. Mabon trying to hide until we go, only we aren't going, so they'll crack before we do."

Mal took Daniel's hand. The grass bank by the wall looked soft and inviting, and they sat down, staring out at the fields below. The farmer had taken the first cut of silage, and the black-wrapped bales were stacked in a pyramid by one of the gates. The river was hidden by a line of trees, and the chainsaws had started up again, the sound drifting towards them on the breeze. Daniel leaned against Mal's shoulder, and when he closed his eyes against the sun's glare, he thought of Mal holding him in the night, rather than Andy Carter's death.

"Did Mabon kill them? Or is Jack Wall the body we think is John Edwards?" he asked, "Is that what they're hiding?"

"I don't know. I do know that I want to find Jack Wall, and soon." He got his phone out and called the station, asking whoever answered to get as much information as possible about Wall, including when he left the country.

"If he did leave," said Daniel.

In answer, Mal turned Daniel to face him and kissed his neck, licking a track up to behind Daniel's ear, making him shiver.

"Fuck, Maldwyn, where did that come from?" Mal did it again, and Daniel felt himself getting hard.

"We're at work."

"Kiss me then, and I'll stop."

"If I kiss you, I won't want to stop."

"That's what I'm banking on."

Daniel pushed Mal away. "You think there's no one here? Let me tell you, *cariad,* there are eyes *everywhere.* I am not making out with you in the open in the middle of the day. Public indecency."

"That's what John Edwards got done for, or almost. Mind you, if I was going to get done for public indecency, I'd rather it was somewhere like this …" He pulled Daniel into his arms again and sighed.

They stared at the view.

"Do you ever think about having children?" Daniel asked.

"Biological impossibility." Mal answered from behind closed eyelids.

Daniel bit Mal's shoulder. "Seriously."

"Seriously? No. I'd be a terrible father."

Daniel bit him again. Then he started to talk about baby Dafydd, how the baby had felt in his arms and how lovely it was to be smiled at, and about his sister's twins, and how much he was looking forward to Huw and Rhiannon's child. "And you wouldn't be a terrible father."

"I think you're supposed to have a positive role model. I didn't."

"Nor did Huw, but he's doing it. Hector says he's going to do the opposite of everything they did in his family, and he figures that should work for Arwen."

"I'm too old."

"Reading between the lines here, you don't want kids."

"You want the truth? I honestly don't know. After this case? I know even less than I did before. You'd make a great father though. If I had kids, I'd want them with you."

Mal's phone rang with the answers to their questions, or some of them. Jack Wall wrote books, just as James Protheroe had told them. According to Abby, he wrote wildly successful high fantasy, one book a year, under the pen name Jak Law. The next book was due in three months, so, as Abby put it, "Wherever he is, no one cares. Yet." They were waiting on the Border Agency to call them about when Wall had left the country.

"Don't go, boss," Abby said, "Charlie wants a word."

"I'm making progress on child abductions," Charlie said, "should have something when you get back."

They gave themselves another five minutes to take in the view, and then got to their feet and headed back to the car.

* * *

Common sense says that Dafydd is either an Edwards, or the child of one of the hippies.

Daniel had believed John Edwards senior, when he denied knowing anything about a third child, and he didn't believe a word any of the hippies said. Charlie knocked at his office door and let himself in. Daniel sat up in his chair.

"Three candidates, boss, and most likely two, because one of them has an Iranian father and he's threatened to take the child there before. Jonsey gave me a hand, fair play, it's not all my efforts."

"OK, talk me through them and let's have a look at the pictures."

Charlie passed a sheaf of photographs over the desk. All showed dark haired toddlers resembling baby Dafydd.

"This is Zack Porter," said Charlie, "parents split six months ago, both have problems with drink and drugs, so Zack was in foster care.

Mum seemed to be back on track, passed all her drugs tests, visited regularly, started taking her son to the park, sometimes on her own, sometimes with a friend. Always came back to the foster carers on time. Until a few months ago, when she didn't. Hasn't been seen since."

Daniel looked hard at the pictures.

"I'm not sure it's him." Daniel reached for the other set of pictures, "It's hard to tell, so tell me about this one."

"Harry Bell. Mother, Monica Bell, has sole custody and there's an injunction against the father to keep him away. He turned up four months ago, grabbed the baby, and when the mother tried to grab him back, knocked her out. Gave her quite a beating. By the time the local police started looking, he'd been gone for hours."

"Whereabouts?"

"Harry Bell in a village near Exeter, Zack Porter in East London."

Daniel thought, Exeter, in *Devon*. Where Mabon had lived before moving to Gelli.

"What's Harry's dad's name?" he asked, and somehow the answer wasn't a surprise.

"Mark Rickard," said Charlie. "It's him, isn't it? Michael Richardson, Mabon ap Richard."

"We'll need to be careful though," Daniel said, "If we tell the mother that we've found him and it isn't him, we'll make it all ten times worse ... let's start by showing these pictures of the mother to little Dafydd and seeing if he recognises them."

Charlie emailed the pictures to Daniel's phone, while Daniel called Veronica and agreed to meet at the carer's house.

Daniel's heart lifted as soon as he saw the little boy, and got his favourite big smile and cry of "Man!" He wanted Dafydd to go home, to find his family again, but he knew he'd miss seeing those smiles. Dafydd ignored the printed pictures in favour of the much more exciting phone screen. Daniel scrolled through until he came to a picture of baby Harry with his mother.

"Mum, mum, mum! More mum!" Dafydd tried to grab the phone from Daniel, shouting, bouncing and then bursting into angry tears when Daniel didn't let go.

"Harry?" Daniel asked, "is that Harry and Mum?"

"Mum!" cried the little boy, reaching for the phone again. "Mum!"

* * *

Jamie thought that he would try to see the luscious DCI Kent one more time before he left, but when he got to the police station the door was blocked by men with television cameras and microphones covered in fur. Jamie had seen the news the night before, and realised that the dead family must be Kent's case. There was no way Ethan's letter was going to take any kind of priority over a famous footballer killing his entire family. He decided to leave the policeman a message, and get back to Cardiff.

The bus to Wrexham station involved a lot of steep hills, twists and turns and some stunning scenery. The hills looked as if they were covered in green velvet, dotted with sheep, and lambs getting big enough for Jamie to start worrying about their fate. The bus stopped in what advertised itself as the highest village in Wales. He felt as if he could've seen as far as Liverpool on a clear day. As it was, what he saw were hills, half hidden valleys, ancient trees and the occasional glimpse of water in the valley bottoms. The land looked prosperous and well cared for.

On the train, Jamie got Ethan's letter out again. He tried to read it as if he was a detective. What did he need to know about the events that led up to the two deaths? He could talk to the two boys' families, find out who their friends were, find out why they were working as sex workers, find out if they were taking drugs, and see if they had left anything behind, like a note. He had three weeks before he needed to re-join the ship in Southampton, and he thought that would be plenty of time. Then he'd hand it over to DCI Kent. There wasn't much of a gay scene in Cardiff, but what there was he knew about. He had a vague idea that there should've been some kind of inquest or enquiry into the boys' deaths, and he had no idea how to find out about that. But their friends? Their family? That he could do. He made a list on his phone, and then he called DCI Kent and told him what he planned.

Jamie had expected a bit of pushback, but not to be told to leave completely alone, in a voice that reminded him of his mother when he'd been naughty.

"Three people are dead, Jamie," said Kent, "I know that they killed themselves, but a lot of people want to keep the lid firmly on those cases. Some of those people are prepared to be violent. Seriously, it's dangerous. Keep out of it."

"But you said you'd help," said Jamie.

"And I will, but not until we dealt with the murders of four people here. I need to be sure that you're not going to get involved."

Jamie wasn't sure that he could give that promise, not without his fingers crossed behind his back. So that was the promise he gave.

Chapter 13

They had all broken their vows. Put excitement and bodily comfort above the promises they had made to each other.

The Border Agency called them back. There was no record of Jack Wall leaving the country. Abby made them check and double-check every possible date but the answer was always the same.

"Sorry, boss, it looks like he is still here. He doesn't have a car, in fact he hasn't even got a driving license. I called his publisher, and they told me who his agent is and she says they haven't heard from him in months. Frantic would be a good description."

Daniel asked if the agent had been to visit the house, and Abby said yes, but got no answer to their knocking.

"Then I think we'd better go and have a look," he said, "If someone was worried enough to come up from London, maybe there really is something to worry about."

Mal had been updating Superintendent Hart while Daniel was talking to Abby.

"It looks like we have to go back to Gelli," Daniel told him, "Because this Jack Wall seems to have disappeared off the face of the Earth."

Mal nodded. "The press are getting very pushy," he said, "and the powers-that-be are putting pressure on Hart for a result."

"Maybe the powers-that-be have a way of finding a missing man in the Berwyn mountains, or a way of getting that bunch of hippies to tell us the truth. Until then, they can butt out."

Daniel said that he thought they'd found Dafydd's mother, and that she was coming to Melin Tywyll as soon as she could get here.

"And how do you feel about that, love?"

Daniel didn't answer, he couldn't. He wanted what was best for the child, but he couldn't help the pangs of jealousy he'd felt when the boy saw the picture of his mother. Too many of his other preoccupations were painful, but his time with the child had been different.

"So that's why you were talking about children this morning?"

Daniel didn't answer that either. His feelings about the little boy were confused and confusing. He didn't trust himself not to cry if he told Mal about Megan's plans. Instead he said "Car keys. Back to Gelli we go."

Daniel enjoyed driving Mal's sleek black Audi, but he still missed his old Land Rover, the mobile skip. Since he'd been drugged and driven the Land Rover into the river, Mal had taken him to see every kind of four-wheel-drive vehicle, but nothing felt right. His insurance company and the police mechanics said there was no hope for the old Land Rover. He looked at adverts for used Defenders, but none of them seemed right either. In the meantime they used Mal's car and Daniel laughed every time he dropped a crumb on its pristine interior.

* * *

There were no signs of life anywhere in Gelli. All the houses looked empty, even though they knew that at least James Protheroe would be at home, and it was only a couple of hours since they'd left the hippies.

They tried the door of number five, went round to the back and tried the back door too. Both were locked. All the downstairs curtains were closed. There was no smell of decay, but somehow that wasn't reassuring.

"He could just have gone off somewhere," said Daniel, "but why didn't he tell someone? He must've had a million phone calls and messages. We could find out about his bank account and his mobile phone, but let's be honest we both think he's dead."

In answer, Mal started searching for the spare key, and found it under a heavy plant pot full of raggedy pelargoniums. He put the key in the door and let them in.

"DCI Kent, did you really do that? Without a warrant?"

"I'm sick of this, all this disappearing," Mal said, "Walk-through, touch nothing, and if he's not here, we'll do bank accounts, track his phone and all the official stuff."

The house was on the same plan as number one, where James Protheroe lived, but it didn't smell of cat, stale food, or unwashed clothes. The kitchen was neat and tidy, the bin empty and the cooker, worktops and sink clean. The fridge door was propped open — all preparations someone would make before going away. In the living room, things were also neat — cushions plumped, carpet showing the tracks of the vacuum cleaner. Just as in James Protheroe's house, the living room contained a small sofa and a single armchair. Unlike in James Protheroe's house, the wall dividing the living room and kitchen was lined with bookcases, with the sofa in front of them, and a small desk by the window. A slim laptop was tucked away on a shelf under the desk. Instead of the ancient gas fire, a wood burner stood on a slab of grey slate, with logs stacked around it. A basket held kindling, old newspapers and firelighters.

"There's obviously not that much money in being a bestselling author," said Daniel, "I mean it's a nice enough house, and the view is great, but it's hardly luxurious, and he doesn't even own it."

"Expensive computer though," said Mal, "but, wouldn't he have taken it with him?"

Upstairs was in line with downstairs. The front bedroom had a double bed, the back room, a large chest of drawers, a shoe rack, and a rail of clothes. It was all plain, simple, and with everything put away. The bed had been stripped, the duvet, pillows and blankets folded on top. Daniel knelt and looked under the bed.

"Backpacks and suitcases," he said.

"And there's a thick waterproof coat hanging on the rail," said Mal, "If he went in the winter, he'd have taken it, surely. And we know he didn't fly off to somewhere warm."

"He's still here, in this house," said Daniel, "and I bet I know where they put the body." He did know, with a flash of clarity, where the body was. What he didn't know was who had put it there, or why.

Daniel led Mal back downstairs, and pointed to the sofa. "The body is under the floorboards, there," he said, "No reader blocks access to all their bookcases with a heavy sofa. The armchair should be in the corner with the books, and the sofa should be facing the fire. There will be marks on the carpet where it used to be."

Mal looked, bent over and fingered the carpet. The marks were clear now he looked for them, deep little indentations, that the hoover tracks couldn't obliterate.

"I should have seen it," he said, "Might not be the body though."

"My house is built like this. No damp-proof course, just a void under the floor. This house has two steps up to the front door. Plenty of room for a dead body."

"Let's call the circus and give the press something else to think about."

They left the house by the back door and Daniel made the call. Mal scrolled through the messages on his phone.

"Shit, shit, shit."

Daniel looked over. Mal was walking away from him, towards the path to the front of the house, jabbing at his phone.

"Do not do any of those things. None of them. Don't ask questions, don't try to see any of their friends, nothing. If you go clubbing, go to get laid, no other reason. Do not say that Ethan left you a letter. Do you understand me?"

"What?" Daniel asked, although he thought he knew the answer.

"Jamie Maddocks doesn't think I'm going to do anything about those boys who killed themselves. So he's going to ask questions, find their friends, talk to their families. He's called twice and won't listen when I tell him to leave it alone."

"You've told him it's dangerous?"

"Of course I have. More than once. Don't be as stupid as him." Mal turned away sharply, his body so tense that Daniel thought he could see vibration. Daniel decided to try empathy.

"He must know you can't drop everything here."

Mal shrugged, still with his back to Daniel.

"You need to go and meet Dafydd's mother," he said, "say goodbye to your fantasy baby. I'll wait here."

Daniel tried to think of a response, but before he could get his mind to function, Mal had thrown him the car keys and was talking on the phone again.

He smiled automatically at the PC staffing the roadblock and ignored the two or three reporters who would soon have something else to write about. He kept replaying Mal's words in his head. *Fantasy baby.* He was numb.

Just do the job.

He went back to the office and shuffled paper until it was time to meet Harry's mother.

* * *

Monica Bell was a small woman with long dark hair. She looked as if she hadn't eaten or slept for months. She hardly looked like the same woman in the photographs that they'd shown to the baby, but that didn't stop her picking up the child and hugging him so hard that Daniel worried for both of their ribs. Daniel had been entranced by the little boy's smile, but the smiles he'd had were pale imitations of the way Harry's face lit up as he saw his mother. If there had been any remaining doubt about the boy's identity, it blew away in that moment. Daniel's eyes filled with tears, and he heard a lot of sniffing and swallowing and saw handkerchiefs produced from handbags and pockets. There weren't many moments like this in his job.

A Devon police officer had driven Monica to Melin Tywyll. Daniel knew that both the police and social services had checked that Monica was who she said she was, and that the courts had given her sole custody of Harry.

Five adults and a toddler didn't leave much room in Mary Kelly's kitchen, but they shuffled round. Monica produced Harry's birth certificate for Veronica, who grinned like the Cheshire Cat as she formally handed Harry back into his mother's care.

"I just want to take him home," Monica said, her chin resting on top of Harry's head, tears falling unnoticed into the boy's hair, "but Mark knows where we are, so I'm going to Holyoak for a bit. It's a housing co-op and I've got friends there I can stay with. He won't dare come there."

Daniel had a lot of questions for Monica, but now wasn't the time. He stuck to the two things they needed most.

"Mabon — Mark — has disappeared with two boys. Do you know where he might have gone? Anywhere he talked about, any relatives he

111

might be staying with?"

Monica shook her head, "Sorry, no."

"Have a think about it, and ring if anywhere occurs to you." Monica said she would. Daniel asked her about Mike/Mark/Mabon's name changes, and whether she knew which was the right one, if any of them were.

Monica laughed. The laughter of someone for whom everything has come right.

"I knew him as Mike and Mark," she said, and laughed again, "Mike when he lived at Holyoak and Mark when I met him again." Then she blushed. "He told me that he was an undercover cop, and I believed him." Monica shook her head and looked down at her son's hair. "I thought it was sexy, until he came for Harry and beat me up. I'm so stupid. All those poor women duped by actual undercover cops, and I fall for a guy *pretending* to be one."

Daniel saw that Harry had fallen asleep on Monica's lap.

"He's a lovely child," he said, "I've only known him for a couple of days, but I'm going to miss him. I can't imagine how it must have been for you."

"Come and visit anytime," Monica said, and Daniel thought that he wanted to, and anyway he did have more questions.

Harry woke up and cried "Beh!" Mary passed him the teddy bear that Daniel had bought him, and this time it was Daniel who blushed. Monica fished in her bag, and produced an identical bear, older and more chewed, but definitely the same animal.

"Snap," she said.

"You can't have too many teddies," said Mary.

Harry looked round. "Bye," he said he pointed at Daniel, "Man. Bye."

"Time to go," said Monica, "once he starts saying *bye* like that, there's a meltdown coming." But her face was full of love, and she held on to her son as if she would never let him go. She looked at Veronica,

Mary and Daniel, and her eyes were bright again with tears.

"Thank you. Thank you so much."

"Bye," said Harry, with a wave.

Veronica asked him to hang on while she signed a form for Mary, and she'd give him a lift back.

"Mary's right. You were good with the baby," she said. Daniel's heart felt heavy.

"Maybe," he said, "but I'm pretty sure Mal doesn't want kids, and this job ... you know how it is." Saying any more would feel disloyal.

"You're close to your nephew and niece though?"

Daniel couldn't help himself.

"They're leaving," he said, "going to spend a year in Spain. They didn't even tell me. Dave's got a job."

Veronica pulled the car into a space by a bus stop.

"That sucks, why wouldn't they tell you?"

"Because they knew I'd be upset, I guess. But I hardly see the kids now. I'm no reason for them to stay here."

"Maybe Megan has been waiting for you to get settled with someone. My mother goes on and on about my settling down with Sophie, as if it's all she ever needed for a happy life."

"I don't know that we are settled," Daniel heard himself say.

"Because Mal doesn't want children?"

"Because gay men aren't like lesbians," he said with an exaggerated wink, "no removal van on the second date."

"Tell it to the marines. The difference is that women talk about stuff rather than just emoting all over the place and then having make-up sex."

"I talk. Sometimes. I'm talking to you, now. And don't knock make-up sex."

"Honey, it's not me you need to talk to."

"I know." He did know, he was afraid that if he started talking, he'd never stop, and that sometimes sex *was* talking.

"Listen, you did good with that child. If you thought it was hard saying goodbye to him, try being a social worker. At least Harry is going back to a decent home, where his father won't find him."

"I'd be more certain of that, if we could actually find his father."

When Veronica dropped Daniel off at the police station, there was a message waiting, *see Spt Hart.*

"Ma'am?" he asked at her office door.

"CSIs found a body in number five Gelli Terrace. Where you said it would be."

So why didn't Mal ring me?

"The Chief Constable has asked DCI Kent to be part of the press conference tonight, appeals for information and, we thought appeals for sightings of Mabon and the two boys."

"Is that wise? People will assume we think he's guilty."

"We know he's guilty of kidnapping his son and beating up his son's mother. We know he's guilty of taking off with two kids, so to be honest, I don't care if people assume that we want to talk to him because he's guilty." Hart took a deep breath. Daniel remembered how she had been at the first briefing, how they had all been. How they all still were whenever they thought about the two little girls.

"But, ma'am, we've got nothing associating him with the deaths of the Edwards family. John Edwards is still the most likely candidate."

"Sorry, Daniel," she said, "I've had John Edwards senior on the phone, and the Chief Constable, and the press office, and it's clear that until those boys are back at home, no one in Gelli will tell the truth. We need to find Mabon, or whatever he's calling himself this week. We need this sorted out, and soon, or the PCC will start wondering whether to call someone else in."

There was a ping from the computer on Hart's desk. She looked at it briefly and a flush spread over her cheeks.

"Revise that last statement. The PCC is already wondering whether to call someone else in."

Chapter 14

H e felt the time ebbing away. There was an escape, and he would take it, he deserved it, but he wanted more time.

Sasha and Arwen had gone to the shop for more ice-cream and Hector was trying to explain to his mother why it was important that she liked Sasha, and made her feel welcome in the family.

"She's a single parent, and she works as a cleaner," he said, "and she's very Welsh. But she's better read than anyone I know, and I love her."

"Who are you trying to convince, darling?"

"You. I don't want you patronising her."

"I shall be perfectly polite to your friend, Hector, as always. I may be a tiny bit offended that you think I wouldn't be."

That's what I'm afraid of, you being perfectly polite.

"Mother," he began, when his phone buzzed and a message from Mal popped up.

"Sorry, I have to go."

His mother didn't sound impressed, but he cut her off anyway. He thought of his mother's *perfect politeness* and how far it could undermine Sasha's confidence. He wanted to chew the phone rather than use it to ring Mal.

"We've found another body. A man. At the end house in Gelli. It looks as if it's been here for a while."

Hector reached for his car keys from the bowl on his desk. Behind it was a photograph from Huw and Rhiannon's wedding — Sasha and Arwen holding hands, in their Jane Austen dresses, with flowers in their hair. They looked as if they had stepped straight out of a BBC2 period drama, exactly the effect Rhiannon was aiming for. After the picture had been taken, Arwen had run off to play with the other children, and he and Sasha had started by talking about dead bodies and finished up making out in a quiet corner. He sent her a text: *duty calls again, love you, x.* Because he did.

* * *

"I don't think we need to look very hard for the cause of death," Mal said, to Hector and Paul Jarvis, as the three of them looked down at the body, "although I suppose someone could have poisoned him before they smashed his head in."

"Or stabbed him," said Hector, "but whatever, no one survives a head injury like that."

"It looks as if someone whacked him with a spade."

"No. Not a spade." Hector looked at the hole where the body lay. Floorboards were piled up against the bookcase, and they had stepped over the section of carpet that the CSIs had cut away. The other side of the room had been busy with paper-suited figures, but they'd moved on, leaving a dust of fingerprint powder, but not much more disturbance.

"There would have been blood, and lots of it," Hector said, "Head injuries bleed." He allowed his eyes to glaze over as he looked around the room, visualising the dent in the dead man's head. His gaze settled on the wood burner, its sharp steel edges a far better fit for the injury

117

than a spade. He touched Mal's arm and pointed.

Mal looked at Paul Jarvis. Jarvis called one of the CSIs back. "Test the stove and the fireplace for traces of blood."

"I'm sure I'm right," said Hector, "and if I am, it might have been an accident. Deliberately pushing someone so they hit their head ... not easy."

"Lifting those floorboards and moving the furniture to cover them up, wasn't an accident though," Mal replied.

* * *

Daniel watched the press conference on the monitor in the CID room. Mal was as skilled as the Chief Constable at giving nothing away. They asked for the public's help in locating Mabon, without saying why they wanted to find him. They glided around the questions about the Edwards family and their deaths. No mention was made of Jack Wall, though the journalists had seen the mortuary van, and knew there must be another body. Seeing him like this, one step removed, Daniel saw Mal as other people must see him, not as the familiar person to cuddle with on the sofa, but a very good looking man, in an expensive suit, dealing with difficult questions like the professional he was. Daniel ached with the fear that Mal was slipping away from him, that he was being pulled back to his quest to save Ethan Maddocks.

It's too late for Ethan. Please don't leave me.

Afterwards, Mal came upstairs and stopped at Daniel's office door. He was wearing the tie with the tiny rainbows. He took his jacket off, stepping backwards to put it on a table in the main office, keeping a distance between them. Mal loosened the tie and rolled his shirt sleeves up. Daniel saw the black hair, and wanted to touch it, wanted to feel Mal's arms around him, because if they were touching, it would mean the awkwardness between them was gone.

"Those journalists are like sharks circling their prey." Mal said, "One sign of weakness and they're on you. I'm starting to understand why John Edwards hid himself away in Gelli."

Daniel thought that they had done well to keep the press away from the hippies and James Protheroe, although he doubted they would succeed for much longer. James Protheroe would talk to anyone. He tuned back in to Mal.

"If Mabon's still out there tomorrow, we're getting the helicopter out to look for him," Mal was saying, "And you were right about the body, though Hector isn't sure he was murdered." Mal told Daniel about the head wound and Hector's thoughts about the wood burner. "When they sprayed for blood, they found it, in the mortar around the fireplace, but someone did a pretty thorough clean up. There was a rug underneath the body, probably from in front of the fire. It was soaked in blood. The CSIs haven't found many fingerprints. So that was my afternoon. How was yours?"

Daniel hesitated. He wanted to tell Mal what Monica had said about Mabon, but he didn't want to talk about the baby, to risk opening himself up for any more barbed comments.

"Monica Bell says Mabon told her that he was an undercover cop, and that's why he kept changing his name," he said in the end. Mal didn't move, staying by the door, not willing to come any closer, but unwilling to turn away altogether.

"I'm sorry for what I said to you," Mal said, "I've got no excuses."

Daniel knew that the social cue was for him to say that it was OK, but he didn't take it.

"About the baby I mean."

"I know what you meant. I don't want to talk about it. I've had a message that the Edwards family is coming here in the morning to identify the bodies, and there are more messages asking someone to call Jack Wall's agent."

"I'll do that," Mal said, "I'll do it now. And then home?"

"Sure."

We are going to have to talk about it, but I don't want to. I don't want you to tell me that we will never have children, or that I'm silly for thinking about it, because a little boy smiled at me.

Daniel didn't know if he did want children, or if his feelings about baby Harry were a reaction to Megan's news. But he'd tried to tell Mal about those feelings, and Mal had used them to hurt him.

* * *

"I'm going to London in the morning, to talk to Wall's agent. Seven o'clock train from Wrexham," Mal said, "She's known him for ten years, and she sounds devastated." He was driving them home. Dread coiled in Daniel's guts about the evening ahead. He thought of all the displacement activities he could try — making something complicated for dinner, putting a movie on, working in the garden — anything so that he didn't have to deal with Mal's stubborn determination to follow up on Ethan Maddocks's letter, and his own conflicted emotions about Megan, baby Harry, the possibility of Hector moving, and the way Andy Carter's death was haunting his dreams.

"Bread and cheese," said Mal when Daniel asked him what he wanted for dinner, "and lettuce and pea shoots from the garden. Which I will get." Then he put his arms out, and Daniel stepped into them without thinking, because he wanted to feel Mal's warmth, despite their argument, and despite the heat of the evening. Because being held, he could try to forget. Mal ran his hands up and down Daniel's back, digging his fingers into the flesh of Daniel's shoulders until Daniel groaned with pleasure and pain.

"You're so tense, love."

"Mmmm."

Mal loosened Daniel's tie and slipped it over his head, then unbuttoned his shirt.

"Come and sit outside, and I'll bring you a beer and give you a shoulder rub."

Daniel thought the cold beer would hiss as it went down his throat, and Mal's hands on his shoulders and neck were divine. A physiotherapist had once tried to loosen his shoulder muscles, only to give up in despair, saying that the permanent tension must be what held him together. He reached around his back, and pointed to a spot below his right shoulder blade that had formed itself into a knot. Mal pressed it hard until it began to soften.

"I'm going to melt into a puddle," he groaned. No amount of painkillers or stretching could achieve this feeling of blissful loosening. Mal shrugged.

"All part of the service. I'll get some more beer."

Daniel's phone rang. He picked it up, saw the call was from Megan and turned it off.

Mal brought beer, bread and cheese and continued the massage.

"Who was on the phone?"

"No one. We should eat."

As well as the bread and cheese, Mal produced strawberries, their first of the year. Not as good as home grown, but *strawberries*, warm and soft and red and syrupy. Not the cold, polystyrene imitations, flown in from who knows where, for people who bought strawberries in December, and didn't understand why they were so hard and tasteless.

The bats began to flit across the sky, too quick for Daniel to focus on before they were gone. The birdsong sounded as if it were coming from far away, loud, but from high in the trees, bird families singing to each other and leaving the insects to the bats. He could hear the rumble of a heavy tractor, making silage, or perhaps hay, while the good weather lasted. The farmers would go on with lights once it went dark. If he and Mal stayed outside, they would hear the owl. If there was a better time of year, Daniel couldn't think of it.

"I don't want to talk about babies," said Daniel, after the fourth beer had combined with the scent of trees, the massage and the evening, to make saying what was in his mind seem possible.

"OK. But I was out of order, and I'm sorry. It was a crap thing to say."

"I don't want to talk about Ethan or Jamie either."

"Can I tell you one thing?"

"Tomorrow. You can tell me tomorrow."

"OK."

"Veronica says men don't talk, they just emote and have make-up sex."

"I like Veronica a lot, but she talks rubbish sometimes."

"You don't want make-up sex?"

"I want to sit here and let it go dark, and then I want to go to bed and for you to fuck me until I beg for mercy, so that I have something to think about on the train tomorrow."

A hot flare of desire flooded Daniel's body. He sat, and allowed anticipation to take the place of the sorrow that had been eating away at him, until darkness fell and it was time to move to the next part of the programme.

If we could just let our bodies talk, everything would be OK.

* * *

Daniel met John Edwards senior at the mortuary in Wrexham. Mrs Edwards and Catherine waited in the car, both of them in the back seat, holding on to each other.

Daniel imagined having to identify the bodies of his family, and shuddered inside.

They began with Hayley. She had an aunt, but hadn't seen her for years, so the task fell to her father-in-law. The mortuary assistant uncovered Hayley's face, framed by the dark hair.

"That's my daughter-in-law, Hayley," said Edwards in a firm voice.

Daniel had already explained that it wasn't possible to identify John Junior from his face, so they showed his father the hand with John's wedding ring, and a twisted copper bracelet that they had taken from the body. Edwards lifted his son's hand. The hand looked waxy and had a blueish tinge, but Edwards held it as if his own warmth could make his son's blood flow again and turn the hand back to pink living flesh.

"That's Hoppy, I mean John. We've called him Hoppy since he was little. Couldn't keep still you see." His voice was still strong, but the slump of his shoulders betrayed him.

"The children were asleep, drugged, we think," said Daniel, "They didn't suffer."

Edwards straightened his shoulders and said he'd be fine. But the sight of the body of his granddaughter undid him. Daniel led him to a chair and asked Abby to bring him a cup of water. He sipped, and gathered himself again, to identify both the children.

"Hop loved those girls," he said, "that's why they moved, to protect them. He wouldn't have harmed them, never in a million years." His voice cracked, and he swallowed hard, tipping his head back as if to hold back the tears.

Daniel noted that no claim was made about not harming his wife, but that was for later.

Abby went to collect Mrs Edwards and Catherine from the car, and they borrowed an office from the hospital administration so that they could talk. Edwards put his arms around his wife and daughter.

"It's them," was all he said. Daniel and Abby left them alone whilst they went to the canteen for coffee and cakes.

"Sugar," said Abby, "it's your answer to everything, boss."

"Don't knock it, young grasshopper," Daniel said, "Millions of bees can't be wrong. Anyway, it's sugar *and* caffeine."

Neither was going to work for the Edwardses. Daniel could see that they were a handsome, affluent-looking couple underneath the ravages of grief. John Edwards wore a dark suit and tie, because he was the kind of man for whom informal clothes wouldn't seem right, except at home. Mrs Edwards's clothes were also formal, but her face was sketched in charcoal — black lines and shadows. Both of them looked as if they had shrunk, flesh scraped away by grief. To give them time to collect themselves, Daniel began by asking Catherine when she'd last spoken to her brother.

Catherine was tall and dark-haired like her brother and her sister-in-law. She'd been crying, and smudged her makeup, but she looked healthy and athletic underneath the misery.

"I spoke to him on the phone before we left for the cruise," she said.

"How did he seem?"

"No different than usual. He teased me a bit about going on *an old people's holiday*, and asked if I was husband-hunting." She smiled — sadly — at the memory. "We got on well, Inspector, but we didn't see a lot of each other, a couple of times a year, if that. My job is pretty full on, and I coach a girls' football team. It's hard to get away."

Don't apologise to me. I'm in no position to judge sibling behaviour. Daniel thought.

"We had hoped that Hoppy and Hayley would come to live in Worcester when they came back from the US," said John senior, "but they wanted somewhere no one would know them. No press attention."

"Hoppy hated the press," said Catherine, "when he was a footballer, and ... did you know he'd been arrested?"

Daniel said that he did.

"They never left him alone after that, and it was bad enough before. It was like they were under siege. There were always journalists trying to get stories, trying to talk to the neighbours, find out if Hop was gay, take pictures of the girls ..."

"Were they happy in Gelli, do you think?"

Catherine looked at her parents. The borrowed office had an obscured glass wall on one side, and Daniel could see movement in the corridor beyond, blurred figures, trolleys with patients and trolleys with tea. Across the table, Daniel could see the struggle on Catherine's face.

"Was it a good marriage?" he asked.

"My brother was very committed to his family," Catherine replied.

"That's not quite what I asked," Daniel said, trying to keep his voice low and calm, hoping that Catherine would tell him the truth, even if it presented her brother as someone capable of killing his family.

"I don't think that they were always happy," Catherine conceded, "Hoppy was arrested with another man, and I wondered ..."

"But there are no out gay professional footballers," said Abby.

Catherine nodded, but her parents looked blank and miserable, as if this was something that came up too often, and that they didn't want anything to do with. Daniel heard James Protheroe calling Jack Wall *a bit of a pansy* and he wondered too.

"Had anything changed recently?" Daniel asked, looking at all of them, knowing that the question was loaded.

Catherine looked at her parents, anxiety making her eyes look huge.

Chapter 15

H e wasn't sure he could trust his own senses, his emotions, his memories. Who was the woman? What did she want?

Mal found the literary agent's office easily, allowing himself to walk there from Euston, instead of taking the tube. He loved the buzz of the city, though the air was a soup of filthy particles of pollution, hanging in water molecules, turning his sweat black. Since the congestion charge, London traffic moved faster, Tottenham Court Road no longer a stop-start jam of vehicles. Cyclists whipped alongside buses, taxis, and the expensive cars owned by people who could afford to pay for the privilege of driving in the city. It felt like coming home.

He'd expected a literary agent called Cynthia Trown to be a white-haired, ex-bluestocking. When they'd spoken on the phone, he'd picked up on the private-school-and-Oxbridge accent, and Cynthia wasn't a young woman's name. But the woman who came to greet him as he got out of the lift was thirty-something, with spiky pink hair and a *very* short skirt. Short enough that she needed cycling shorts underneath to keep it decent.

The agency was in an undistinguished office block, with its entrance in an alley between a Primark and a Superdrug. A few fans and portable air conditioners stood around, in a big space filled with desks, not making much impact on the heat and humidity. The walls were covered with paintings of dragons in fantastical landscapes, misty mountains, and distant towers. Low tables were piled with paperbacks, covers featuring sword-wielding maidens, or shirtless men resting their hands on a crystal, or a wolf's head. A fountain played in one corner, water falling into a bowl of blue glass pebbles. Mal felt overdressed in his suit and tie, as well as far too hot.

Cynthia led him to a glass-walled meeting room, and offered coffee. When he said yes, she leaned out of the door and shouted for someone called Paris to bring their drinks.

"I can't believe this is happening," she said, "Jack is one of our stars, and he's my friend … dammit," Cynthia ran out of the door and came back with two coffees and a box of tissues.

"Sorry. I can't stop crying," she blew her nose and gave a watery smile, "It's making work pretty difficult. Hard to talk to one author when I'm crying over another. Doesn't make people feel loved. It's not just me, we're all in shock. Aren't you hot?"

Mal took his jacket off and put it over a chair. It helped, but did nothing to stem the flow from Cynthia.

"Have you read any of Jack's books? I know I'm paid to say how good they are, but in his case it wasn't hard. Not many people make a living from writing one book a year, not in this genre, but Jack could. He wasn't a millionaire, far from it, but he loved his little house, and the freedom he had, sorry, am I going on? It's my worst habit, well, one of them. I'll shut up and let you ask your questions."

Faced with the torrent of words, Mal struggled to organise his thoughts into a series of questions. He fell back on one that he thought would set Cynthia off again, so he could grab some coherence from his coffee.

"How well did you know Mr Wall?"

Cynthia blushed bright red, a colour that didn't sit well with the pink hair. Then she burst into noisy sobs and buried her face in a pile of tissues. "Sorry," she kept saying as another paroxysm of tears overtook her. Mal's coffee was gone by the time the storm passed. Cynthia blew her nose once more, took a mouthful of cold coffee and pulled a face. She opened the door and called for Paris. A very young woman appeared, surely still at school, thought Mal.

"Paris, love, two more coffees, and could you find the paracetamol in my top drawer?"

She turned to Mal.

"I liked Jack a lot. He's been on our books from the beginning. My boss handled him at first, but when I started, she said I should take over. We wanted him to write more, because we can sell anything he does. Chez - that's my boss - thought someone younger might persuade him."

"But you couldn't?"

"Nope. He wasn't interested. Said as long as he could live on one book a year, that was all he wanted to do. He did a few festivals, and signings, and he was really good about reading other authors' stuff for review quotes, but he was as stubborn as a mule when he didn't want to do something. It's like he had a quota in his head — so many things he'd turn up at, so many reviews, and when he'd done them, he said no, and that was it. His sales were so good that we didn't have any leverage, and he knew it."

There was a knock at the door and Paris came in with their coffee and a box of painkillers for Cynthia. She swallowed them dry, a skill Mal envied. The coffee was in big mugs, decorated with the fantasy scenes that covered every other surface. He asked his next question.

"What about his personal life, his family?"

The blush came back, though not the tears.

"You were more than friends, you and Jack?" Mal asked gently. It would explain why Cynthia had been to Wales to visit, when Jack had dropped out of sight, though if there had been a relationship, it was very long distance.

Cynthia rubbed her face with a new tissue, running it underneath her eyes and examining the remains of her mascara.

"I must look a sight."

Mal shook his head, and waited.

Cynthia gave a crooked smile.

"I suppose you'd say we had a fling. Friends with benefits. If we went to the same festival, or he came to London. It's embarrassing. I kept hoping it would come to something, but it wasn't going to. I knew that really. My friends say he's a user, and maybe they're right ..."

"Did you visit his home in Gelli?"

"Once." Cynthia's face twisted at the memory. "Afterwards I wondered if all he wanted was a lift home. We'd been at a festival in Manchester, and he kept saying how there was no decent public transport where he lived, and I had the car, because I had all the books ... because once we got to his house, he obviously wanted me to go ... God, this is so humiliating."

Mal thought that there was more to come and he was right.

"I'd made my mind up to tell him, no more, but it was too late. He'd already found my replacement." For the first time, Cynthia sounded bitter.

"What did he say?"

"He said that his next book would have romance, because he was in love. I was such a dope. I thought it was me. Only for a second, then he said *so no more lovely dalliances, sweet Cynthia.*"

Mal fumed silently on Cynthia's behalf, whilst wondering whether she had gone up to Wales to take her revenge. He hoped not, he was coming to like Cynthia more than he liked the sound of Jack Wall.

"Did he say who this person was? The one he was in love with."

"No. I put the phone down. I felt like the worlds biggest fool. I rang him back later, but we just talked about books. I never asked about this woman."

"Could it have been a man?"

Mal almost laughed as Cynthia's head tipped to one side, a classic illustration of the body language of thought. He could see the cogs turning as she processed the idea.

"Maybe. Jack never said he was bi, and none of my gay friends ever suggested it, but he could be pretty camp, and well, no stereotypes, but he was always very clean and he did like clothes. A bit like you in fact." She winked, and this time Mal did laugh.

He couldn't ask Cynthia for an alibi, because they didn't know when Jack died. But he thought that she couldn't have easily hidden her presence in Gelli, not for long enough to lift the floorboards and hide the body, even if she had the strength to do it by herself.

Mal asked for details of Wall's next-of-kin, or any other family information that she had.

"All I know is that he was born and brought up in Glasgow, and went to university in Edinburgh, so his family are up there. He never mentioned them, but then it wasn't that kind of relationship."

He asked her to ring him if she thought of anything useful, and she gave him a signed copy of Jack's last book, "To read on the train." He promised that he would.

Back out in the soupy streets, Mal headed into Soho, weaving his way amongst the crowds, jacket and tie neatly folded in his bag, along with his new book. The narrow pavements were made narrower by tables and chairs, and the sticking out limbs of the people sitting at them. Tall buildings shaded the streets, but provided no relief from the heat. Rainbow flags hung limply above the doors to bars and restaurants.

"Mal!" a voice called from inside the open door of a small bistro. He went in, eyes adjusting to the lower light, and found his friend, and ex-boss, in a quiet corner.

"Chief Superintendent." Mal said, but he was smiling. Jason MacLean was his superior officer, but the two had been friends, and sometimes housemates, since Hendon. Jason was the only Metropolitan police officer who had known for sure that Mal was gay, and he didn't care because so was he. They'd worked some major cases together, and Jason had used every argument at his command to persuade Mal to stay in London.

"How's life in the sticks, then?" Jason asked.

"Plenty of work," Mal replied with a shrug, "I miss this place though."

"Come back," Jason waved at a passing waiter, and asked for beers and menus. "As you so kindly noticed, I've been promoted, so there's going to be a vacancy for a Super. I'll be interviewing."

"I've met someone. In North Wales. He's settled there."

"A copper?"

Their beers came, condensation running down the sides of the bottles. They chinked their bottles together.

"Cheers," said Jason, "is he a copper, this bloke?"

Mal nodded, "DI, promotion long overdue."

"Bring him with you. Always jobs for good detectives, you know that."

He wouldn't come. Won't leave his sister, won't leave his trees.

"Like I said, he's settled where we are."

"He must be pretty special, this guy, if he can keep you in the country you told me you hated, and away from a promotion I can as good as guarantee."

"He is." *Because if he wasn't, I'd be on the first train out.*

The waiter came back with an expectant expression. They looked at their menus and chose.

"Come on, Mal, this is the friend equivalent of a *No Comment* interview. Do you live with him, are you both out at work, what's he like?"

In answer, Mal took out his phone and showed Jason a picture he had taken of Daniel at Rhiannon's wedding, smiling and relaxed, white linen shirt crumpled, hair sticking up, blue eyes shining over the champagne glass he was holding out.

"Ah," said Jason, "now I get it."

"He has a smallholding outside the town he grew up in. Grows his own food. Built his own house. His first language is Welsh, and he knows everyone, and everyone likes him. The locals put up with me because of him. He's been out since he was at school. Small town, nowhere to hide."

"You could commute."

"Believe me, I've thought about it." Mal shrugged, "It wouldn't work in this job. No, I'm stuck, sorry, mate."

Their food arrived and they ate, catching up on news of mutual friends and old enemies, inside and outside the job. Mal talked about the killings in Gelli, and Jason about dealing with the threat of terrorism in the capital.

When their plates had gone, they ordered coffee and Mal produced the copy of Ethan's letter.

"I need your thoughts," he said, "this guy, Ethan Maddocks, killed himself after he was raped in the cells."

"You told me," said Jason, "so what's this?"

Mal explained about Ethan leaving the letter for Jamie, and Jamie bringing it to Melin Tywyll, and asking Mal to do something, then threatening to ask questions himself.

"The thing is, Jase, Glamorgan basically told me never to darken their doorstep again. And no way are Glamorgan going to investigate any more sex worker suicides or harassment of sex workers by their own people."

132

"But if you don't do anything, some other scrote will get away with it, and this Jamie kid will get himself in deep shit."

Jason read the letter, and drummed his fingers on the table. Mal drank his coffee, and calculated how long he had before the direct train back to Wrexham.

"Could be the same guys who raped Maddocks, harassed these other kids," said Jason, "in which case, we've already dealt with them."

"Though not for everything they did."

"As you say. But if it was someone else …"

"Or if it's still going on …"

They both knew that it was a bigger problem than Ethan Maddocks, or the boys in Cardiff.

"No one looks out for those kids, Jason, no one."

"You could though, but not from up there in the middle of nowhere. Down here we could set something up. You in charge. Promotion. Think about it. We could do a year's secondment."

Mal didn't want to think about returning to London. He didn't want to think about setting up a unit to target exploiters of the young queer kids who washed up on the streets after their families threw them out. So he got Jack Wall's latest book out of his bag. *City of the Vrystal Lure (Book 15 in the bestselling Vrystal Lure series)*. It wouldn't have been his reading of choice, but Cynthia had assured him that it was a page turner, and that he didn't need to have read books one to fourteen to follow the story. He was curious to see if she was right. She wasn't, or at least, not for him. He didn't hate it, but he couldn't face the whole four hundred pages. It was a signed copy, so he would take it into the station in case anyone was a fan.

He looked at the information about the author — nothing he hadn't already learned from Cynthia — and at the acknowledgments.

First, as always, thanks to my parents Callum and Chrissie for their endless encouragement, and to my agent Cynthia for being the best agent any writer could have. My editor, Barbara is an exacting task mistress, but these books are the better for it. RX Penty has done his usual brilliant job on the cover – thanks mate! I want to thank the many members of my Facebook readers group for keeping me going when the words dry up. Fantastick Books are as fantastic as always, and if you are looking at this book, it's down to their efforts. They are a truly great team.

Finally thanks to HE for bringing new light into my life. The next one is for you.

Chapter 16

He wanted to explain that there had been no choice. The woman listens but she doesn't understand. No one has understood for a long time.

The helicopter clattered overhead, making loops outwards from where Mabon had left the orange camper.

Daniel had left Abby in Wrexham to see what Hector could discover from what was left of Jack Wall, while he and Bethan returned to Gelli. The drive was becoming more familiar, thought Daniel, but it never seemed to get any shorter. The sky was hard blue, against the Van Gogh yellow of the oilseed rape. Haymaking was a constant background noise. No one expected the weather to last.

"Still without a car then, boss," she said, sinking into the luxury of the Audi, "such a hardship having to drive this."

Daniel stroked the padded steering wheel. "We've only got it because Mal wouldn't leave it at Wrexham station all day, so make the best of it. He keeps taking me to see *the perfect thing* but they never are. Perfect, I mean. Shiny, all the bells and whistles, four wheel drive, but not for me. And he won't let me look at secondhand Land Rovers." He pulled an exaggerated sad face and laughed. "How can you miss a *car?*"

"It does seem odd, not seeing the old wreck parked outside the station, but on a day like today, air conditioning beats the hell out of opening the windows, and listening to all the rattling. Why are we going to see these people again?"

Daniel sighed. "Who knows. They only ever tell lies. But we're meeting the Edwardses at John and Hayley's house, so they can look round and see if anything looks wrong — don't worry, we're not letting them in the kitchen. And Paul Jarvis should be finished at Jack Wall's, so we can see him too."

They reached the roadblock, a mobile barrier with a solitary marked car and a very fed-up uniformed officer. A TV van, with a satellite dish on top was parked on the verge, and they had questions shouted at them as the barrier was moved to let them through. Daniel hoped that the reporters wouldn't recognise the Edwardses, and was glad they'd arranged an unmarked police car to bring them to the house.

Paul Jarvis didn't have much to offer.

"All the paperwork, computer, mobile — I'll drop it on your desk. No fingerprints to talk about, it's all been cleaned. A few partials, but nothing to compare them to yet. Whoever did the cleaning wore rubber gloves." He shrugged. Daniel knew Paul preferred to impart bad news — no one could accuse him of being a glass-half-full type of man — but it didn't look like the house had much to tell them. He told Paul that the Edwards family were going to look round *Ty Gelli*. "But not the kitchen."

"No. You've got the number of the cleaning service?" This time Paul's look of unhappiness was one Daniel could sympathise with. "I'll go and pull the blinds closed, and tape up the doors," he said. Daniel thanked him. Even without the two bodies, the kitchen looked like a slaughterhouse. Not something grieving parents should see.

At the hippie house, Cai answered the door with a sour expression. Daniel could see some of the children playing with coloured blocks on the floor behind him, and Mel and Becca in the kitchen.

"Let me guess, just a few more questions. Keep this up, and there won't be anyone left to ask."

"Sorry?" Daniel asked.

"You don't have to talk to him," Mel called from across the room, "just shut the door."

"Before you do," said Daniel, "you need to know that we have a helicopter searching for Mabon and your sons. If you know where they are, you could save us all a lot of trouble."

"Fuck off," said Cai, and slammed the door.

Daniel and Bethan looked at each other, and Daniel could see Bethan struggling not to laugh.

"That's us told," she said, "Sorry, boss, but dead bodies on either side of them, two of their kids missing, and they stand on their rights not to talk to the police? They think *we* are the problem?"

Daniel looked round the area in front of the houses. Something seemed different.

"Radio down to the guy doing the roadblock," he said, "because I think there's another car missing. I'm sure there was an old blue estate, maybe a Ford."

Bethan rolled her eyes, and called. Daniel heard an indignant squawk from the radio.

"No, of course you weren't supposed to stop them leaving," Bethan said, "though it would have been useful to know that they'd gone." More squawking. Bethan clicked the radio off.

"Two of the hippies, with two small children and a car packed full of stuff left first thing. Didn't talk to our guy, just waited for him to move the barrier and drove off. By a miracle, he took the number."

"Fair play, he's there to stop the press getting *in* not the residents getting *out*. I guess that explains what Cai meant about there being no one left to talk to."

"Surely we're going to have to bring them all in for formal interviews?"

Daniel nodded. If they didn't, the residents would scatter. It was a conversation he needed to have with Mal when he got back from London.

Bethan's phone rang. She listened for a moment and then said, "Well, that's how it is. Good luck."

"Someone's fallen off Crib Goch," she said, "we've lost the helicopter." They have sent all the pictures back to the station, but they didn't see anything to get excited about. I'll get someone to go through them anyway." Bethan called the station to set it up, and to look for ANPR traces on Bethany and Tom's car.

They walked over to the low wall surrounding *Ty Gelli* and sat down to wait for the Edwardses.

"This is a dog's breakfast of a case, boss," Bethan said, "Are we looking for a man who killed his family and himself, or a murderer? Is Jack Wall's death related to the Edwards's? Is Mabon a kidnapper or a murderer or both? Or has he just taken those two boys camping?"

"You've forgotten that we don't know where the shotgun came from, and that John Edwards fired it, and that he died hours after the others, and that we don't know when Jack Wall died, only that it may well have been an accident. The only crime we know about for sure, is that Mabon abducted his son Harry, and assaulted the boy's mother."

"But we don't know why the hippies said Harry was called Dafydd, and belonged to the Edwardses."

Daniel had the faintest inkling of an idea about that, but he was afraid that if he looked at it too closely, it would evaporate.

They heard the sound of a car approaching, and stood up. John Edwards senior, his wife and daughter got out, along with PC Jones, who had been their driver.

"Sir, Sarge," he said, "I did my best to run over a few of those journalists, but I wasn't quick enough."

"It was horrible," said Catherine, "poking their cameras against the windows, urgh." She shuddered. "But this is such a beautiful place ..."

They walked towards the front door of the house, Daniel explaining that the kitchen was still a crime scene. He would tell them about the specialist cleaning firm later.

"We'd appreciate you telling us if anything looks different or out of place," he said, "Anything that you don't think belonged to John and Hayley, or if there's anything that you think should be here that isn't."

The downstairs rooms caused no comment, apart from the sharply indrawn breaths at the bloodstain where the dog's body had lain. Marian Edwards picked up the crayons and books that her granddaughters had played with, and laid them down again with such tenderness that Daniel wanted to howl.

Upstairs, they all said that they'd expected the nursery to have been turned back into a bedroom, or a study.

"They only used it for the first year, then they decorated the other room for the girls. Before that, they were both in here," said Catherine, "but they'd have got rid of the cot and so on. I'm surprised there's a cot at all."

Daniel's thoughts turned to his idea about the pretence that Harry belonged to the Edwardses. It was over-complicated, rushed, this attempt to create the impression that he had ever lived in this house. Bethan led the way into the main bedroom. Except that the curtains had been opened, it was as it had been when they first entered, duvet thrown back, pillows with the indentations of people sleeping. John's parents stared, his mother weeping silently. Catherine idly opened the doors of the built in wardrobes.

"Mum?" she said, "look." Marian Edwards joined her and they moved some of the clothes on the rail.

"What is it?" Daniel asked.

The wardrobe had built-in drawers, and racks for shoes, as well as multiple hanging rails. Catherine pulled a few drawers out and showed her mother.

"Half of Hayley's clothes are missing," she said, "maybe more. Hayley loved clothes."

"And shoes," said Marian Edwards, "she was always buying shoes."

"She never had enough wardrobe space," said Catherine, "John used to laugh at her, living in the middle of nowhere with shedloads of designer gear. But she said she was saving it all for the girls, or that she needed it for holidays."

"Maybe she had a clear out," said Bethan, "or she's put it in the loft, or in storage."

Daniel shook his head. "There's no paperwork for storage, and the loft was just suitcases. Empty suitcases."

"You didn't know Hayley," said Catherine, "When I say she loved clothes, she *really loved clothes.* No way would she have got rid of any of her things. Anyway, they went to London a couple of times a year, and on holiday. It wasn't all vegetable-growing and finger painting."

Marian Edwards chipped in, "Hayley was one of those women who never got dirty or creased. She could wear a ball gown on a country walk, in winter, and come back without a spot of mud on the hem. No, this wardrobe should be stuffed full."

Bethan joined the two women at the wardrobe, and looked at the labels on the clothes still there. "None of this is cheap," she said, and Catherine gave a snort of laughter, cut off quickly.

"She was a nice woman," Catherine said, "a great mother, and I think she was probably a great nurse too. But I never knew that you could spend five hundred pounds on a pair of jeans until I met Hayley. There are thousands of pounds worth of clothes missing from here, and believe me, she didn't take them to the charity shop."

CHAPTER 16

* * *

Abby didn't enjoy watching the pathologist work. The smell in the mortuary, and the autopsy suite, made her feel sick. The knowledge that behind the doors was what was essentially a fridge full of dead people gave her the creeps. Too many zombie movies she told herself, except that she didn't watch zombie movies if she had a choice. The DI had once told her that he didn't worry about autopsies. What bothered him was what happened to people *before* they died. She'd shivered, and he'd patted her arm. "Don't worry," he'd said, "I'm the odd one out. No one expects you to like watching autopsies. Yet another not-fun part of our job."

Dr Lord was kind and funny, and Abby knew that he always made sure that observers were prepared for anything really gruesome, but this was an examination of the remains of someone who'd been hidden under floorboards for *months.* She was told to take a seat well away from the examination table.

"You can hear what I have to say, and I'll call you if there's anything you need to see," Dr Lord said, "and you can start with this."

This was a small pile of evidence bags.

"The body was fully dressed, and these are the things we found in his pockets. So either our corpse stole Jack Wall's identification, or this is him."

Abby looked through the bags. Bank cards and a library card in the name of Jack Wall, some money, and a few receipts melded into a single shiny lump. Another bag contained a notebook, a small one like she carried in her own pocket. They could compare the handwriting to Wall's, she thought, if the notebook could be opened. Finally, a letter, folded up, and stuck together, but with the plastic window still showing the name and address: Mr J Wall, 5, Gelli Terrace.

141

A little while later, she was called to look at the broken skull. It was horrible, but she did it, and Dr Lord was certain that it was the cause of death, so she could go back to the office with information and a clear conscience.

Armed with the names of Jack Wall's parents, Abby started searching, wondering why there was no missing person's report on their system. Surely, if Wall's agent had missed Jack, his parents would have noticed his absence? The acknowledgments that the DCI had photographed and sent to her from the train, showed that Wall didn't hate his parents, so why hadn't they reported him missing after all this time? Just one more thing about this case that made no sense. And when Abby found Jack's parents it made even less sense than it did before.

She didn't want to make the call to Callum and Chrissie Wall, but there was no one else in the office. She rang the DCI, on the train back from London, to say she'd tracked them down, and heard the tease in his voice as he wondered aloud why she hadn't rung the number already.

"It's the far north of Scotland, sir, some hamlet the size of Gelli, only in Sutherland. Nearest police station is fifty miles away."

"That's no reason not to ring them. Where's the rest of CID?"

"They're all out, sir." She'd assumed that Kent would know where everyone was, that the DI would have told him. She hoped that things were OK between her two bosses, because when they fell out, things had a habit of becoming very tense in the office. Then she decided to stop wondering, pull on her big girl pants, and make the call.

"I think you must be mistaken, Constable Price." Callum Wall had a soft Scottish accent, and sounded very confident that she'd got it wrong. "We haven't seen Jack for a while, but he texts and emails all the time. He's fine."

When Abby asked if Callum had *spoken* to his son, there was a silence. She asked if he would be kind enough to check the date of the last time they had spoken rather than texted or emailed. He said that he would.

Abby rang Kent. She heard the recorded announcement of the *next station stop* from the train's tannoy system and waited until it ended for Kent to speak.

"Wall's computer, and his phone were found in his house in Gelli. Someone has been pretending he was still alive."

* * *

Hector couldn't avoid his mother for ever. If Sasha insisted on meeting her, he had to arrange something, but he quailed. He'd succeeded in keeping his life in north Wales and his family in two separate boxes for years, and it worked, but not for much longer. Answering his mother's call felt like taking a scalpel to the tape holding the boxes closed.

"Darling, there is *the* most lovely spa hotel not far from you. I know it's short notice, but I've booked Ginny and I in for a couple of days and we just arrived. You must bring your friend to dinner."

His mother was bad enough. His sister-in-law was far, far, worse.

"That sounds great. But I'd like to make dinner at my house." His mother began to protest, but if his mother and Ginny came to him, he could ask Daniel and Mal, and Ginny would spend the time ogling Mal rather than condescending to Sasha.

"No, Mother, I insist. You've never seen my house, and you should. The garden is lovely. I'd like you to see it. Come tomorrow night, about six, and have a potter round the garden before we eat."

He thought that might do the trick. His mother liked gardens, and would happily poke around making lists of tasks for him. Something else to take the pressure off Sasha. Now he had to tell Sasha, and

143

persuade Daniel and Mal. And think of something to cook. And buy the ingredients. And make sure that he had enough plates. And chairs. And cut the grass.

That's OK, I have a whole day to get it all done and I'm not supposed to be at work, even if I am.

Chapter 17

*S*he got angry because he'd broken the promises she said he'd made. She wanted money, like they all did, one way or another.

The caller sounded young, very young, and frightened, but the call handler had been trained, so she was patient and gentle.

"Can you tell me your name?"

"Ben Jones."

"OK, Ben, do you know where you are?"

"No, sorry. On a mountain. And there's a fire. I'm really scared."

The call handler saw the pop-up flash on her screen. She waved urgently for her supervisor, and carried on talking to the boy.

"No need to be sorry, Ben, and don't be scared, we'll have someone with you as soon as we can. Can you tell me again what happened? Take your time."

The supervisor gave a thumbs up, and made another call.

Daniel, Bethan, Sophie, and Superintendent Hart stood with Dave Hewitt, the leader of the Mountain Rescue team and looked at the large scale map pinned to the board. Daniel and Bethan had been back in the police station less than a minute, before being called to the briefing room. Dave pointed to a spot on the map, "That's where Ben is," he pointed to another spot, "from what I know, the most likely place for the others to have fallen is somewhere here, or here," They could see the markings of rocks, maybe even a small quarry, on the map, slightly north of Ben's location, and another to the west. Dave traced a route from the nearest road to where Ben was waiting.

"About an hour to walk from the road," he said, "and about half an hour to get everyone together. I've been on to the Fire Service. It's a grass fire, and it's a few miles away, but there's lots of smoke." He turned to Hart, "We'll need everyone you can spare," he said, and Hart looked at Sophie.

"On it ma'am," she said and left.

"Charlie and I will go," said Daniel, and went to tell Charlie to get changed out of his suit.

The Mountain Rescue Land Rover led the way off the main road and up a narrow B road into the hills. They crossed a cattle grid and the road turned into a track. Dry-looking slopes rose up on either side, rising to a small, rocky, top on the left and a more gentle gradient on the right, up the flank of the first of the mountains proper. They bounced along until they reached a stream, not much more than a trickle after the dry weather, but the end of the road for the vehicles. A narrow footbridge led to a walking path, with another path following the stream on their side. By the time PC Morgan had stopped the police 4x4, the Mountain Rescue team were unloading their gear.

In the steep-sided valley, it was hot, though Daniel hoped it would be cooler as they climbed. The mountain ahead of them, Moel Wyn, wasn't high on a world scale, but this was wild and empty country. There were sheep, their lambs gone to market and death, and there were the wild animals — foxes, rabbits, hares, badgers, and all the tiny creatures. Overhead, red kites circled endlessly, using the thermals to soar without effort. A buzzard cried its high scream, and Daniel looked up, but the sky was too bright and the bird was gone.

Paths were indistinct, overgrown with roots and branching into spiders' webs of sheep tracks and empty watercourses that would turn into torrents after rain. Underfoot was dry and dusty, and they had to pick their way, avoiding hidden rocks and rabbit holes. Further ahead there were pockets of native trees, sheltered by folds in the hill. The odd lonely hawthorn leaned away from the prevailing wind, branches fanning out to the east.

Daniel and Charlie carried a stretcher between them. Everyone, police and Mountain Rescue, had equipment to carry, and Dave made them move fast, looking frequently at the smoke blowing in from the west. Charlie complained, because he was Charlie, about his boots, which he claimed were his old street pounding boots, and which he said were giving him blisters.

"You could have had wellies," Daniel said, knowing that Charlie would start to rattle on about sweaty feet in wellies, and he could stop listening and concentrate on keeping up the relentless pace. The terrain made it hard to get into a rhythm, and he could hear his comrades panting with the effort. Only Charlie moaned, but moaning never slowed Charlie down. The sounds of haymaking quieted as they climbed, leaving the buzzards' cries and the rustle of the dry vegetation. There were no pauses to look at the view, and ahead was more of the same, steep, bare slopes stretching into the distance.

Bethan was collecting Mel, Cai and Becca, bringing them to the bottom of the path to meet the rescue party. They could have sent a uniformed officer, or just told them where to come, but Daniel was hoping that one of them would say something helpful. Probably a forlorn hope, he thought, but worth a try.

Suddenly there was a cry from the front. Daniel looked and saw a flash of colour, and Ben was running towards them, waving his arms, slipping on the steep slope until Dave's shouts made him wait. As he got closer, Daniel saw that the boy had been crying. They all stopped and put down their packs. Dave motioned to everyone but the team's medic to keep back, not to crowd round Ben. Daniel got his phone out and called Bethan.

"We've found Ben," he said, "he seems fine." In the background he could hear Bethan talking, and a sob of relief from Becca. "I don't know how long we'll be," he said in answer to Bethan's question, "but I'll let you know."

Dave came back to the group.

"The lad's confused," he said, "but he's OK. Hungry and tired, but OK. He says that the other lad has hurt his foot, and is in their tent, but the adult has fallen and banged his head. I've got an idea where the casualties are, so I think Ben should go down." He looked at Daniel. "Can two of your guys take him back to the cars? He'll probably need a piggy back some of the way."

Daniel nodded at Charlie and PC Morgan. "Ben's mum and dad are waiting for him," he said.

A minute later, they were on their way, Ben munching a chocolate bar and walking, even as his feet dragged and his shoulders drooped. Daniel could see PC Morgan ready to scoop him up and carry him down the mountain.

The rest of the group carried on to the shoulder of Moel Wyn, the path finally flattening out as it contoured around the mountain, a couple of hundred feet below the summit.

"If I'm right," said Dave, "the quarries are just through those trees." Daniel looked and there was a narrow path sloping steeply uphill through the scrub.

"Let me go," said Daniel, dropping his end of the stretcher, and setting off up the path. If Mabon or Josh had fallen far, well, Daniel already had nightmares, no point in anyone else suffering.

I'm paid to look at the damage people can do to themselves.

He burst out of the trees and into a small disused quarry, with a tent pitched close to the the rock face. There was no sign of Mabon or Josh, so he called their names. A whimper came from inside the tent, and Daniel ran over.

"Josh, what's wrong?"

"I think I've broken my foot," Josh said, and as Daniel dropped to his knees to crawl into the tent, Josh burst into tears. "It really hurts ... I thought no one would come ..."

Daniel reached for the boy's hand and squeezed. "We're here, and we're going to take you down to your mum. She's been worried."

"Ben went to get help, but it was so long ..."

"It's OK, shush now, it's OK," Daniel needed to know where Mabon was, but he hated to add to the boy's distress. He asked anyway.

"He slipped. He was helping me and he slipped, and banged his head. Over on the other side, behind some rocks. I didn't know what to do, but Ben helped me and then he took a sleeping bag to keep Mabon warm, and took the phone, only there wasn't a signal. Ben knew what to do." Josh's misery said that he was humiliated at not having known what to do, on top of his pain and exhaustion.

"You did great Josh. We're going to get you home. I'm going to check on Mabon now and I'm calling the others to get you sorted out. There's a doctor. Is that OK?"

Josh nodded, and Daniel squeezed his hand once more and backed out of the tent. At the top of the path, he called to Dave.

"Josh is here, in the tent, he's hurt his foot," and as he heard the team begin to scramble up the path, he went to look for Mabon, fearing the worst. He hadn't liked the guy, but *slipped and hit his head* sounded like bad news.

Without the bright red sleeping bag, Daniel wouldn't have spotted Mabon so quickly. He'd fallen behind a jumble of rocks, a torn patch

149

of still-damp moss showing where he'd slipped. He looked very still, but Daniel felt for a pulse, and it was there, faint, erratic, but *there*. He stood up and shouted, "Over here!"

Dave and Leo, the medic, ran over.

"There's a pulse, Josh said he banged his head when he fell," said Daniel, and moved out of the way, to let Leo take his place. The medic cursed under his breath.

"This is bad," he said, and cursed some more.

Footsteps came up behind them. "The lad's foot is badly sprained, but I don't think it's broken. Needs an X-ray though, to be sure, and he won't be walking down." It was one of the uniformed officers, who Daniel knew was a trained first aider, and as he had discovered earlier, a member of the Mountain Rescue.

Leo turned, "Can you strap it up, Doug, while Dave and I work out how we're going to get this guy out of here?" When they lifted the sleeping bag off Mabon, his body looked twisted in all the wrong ways, bringing more curses from Leo.

Daniel felt like a spare part. He was used to being the one in charge, knowing what to do, and giving instructions. Here he was no more than willing muscle, waiting to be told where to lift. Even asking for instructions meant interrupting someone who did know what they were doing. He was more conscious of the smoke. On the way up the mountain, they'd seen it, but now the smell was stronger, and when he looked at the quarry rim, it seemed thicker and darker.

Dave called them over. Mabon was wearing a neck brace, and an oxygen mask.

"We need him on the stretcher, but no rolling *at all*." As the least experienced of the group, Daniel was given the oxygen cylinder, and very strict instructions not to get in the way. Moving the unconscious Mabon was agonisingly slow, and Daniel couldn't help his awareness of the thickening smoke beginning to catch in the back of his throat.

He wasn't the only one. Dave snapped,

"Daniel, get down to where there's a signal and ring for the chopper. Run." Daniel ran.

It wasn't good news.

"They'll come as soon as they can," he told Dave, "Just now, they're getting people off a sinking boat. Half an hour minimum. And we need to be out of the smoke."

"Shit and double shit." People were starting to cough.

"Let's get the lad out of here." Dave pointed to Daniel and Doug. "Call the people at the bottom, get them coming up and get down to meet them. Then come back and help with the stretcher. Go."

They went, holding Josh between them in a "chair" made of slings. Doug handed Daniel a rucksack marked "Ropes", and swung another one onto his own shoulders.

"Just be glad Josh here is a bit of a lightweight." He grinned at the boy, who was still subdued.

"Don't worry, Josh, you'll be back down to your mum in no time," said Daniel, and he wondered at Josh's quietness.

The others picked up the stretcher, with Leo holding a drip and the oxygen bag, beside them. The steep path down through the trees was treacherous. Doug told Josh to hold on to them as tightly as he could, and kept up a teasing banter, with horrible jokes until Josh finally smiled.

Back onto the main path, the smoke was less dense, blowing towards them, but not getting trapped as it had been in the quarry. They had a few minutes of almost level ground, and then it was time to head downhill.

"Hold on tight, it's gonna be a bumpy ride," Doug said and the three of them began to slither down the slope towards the stream.

"Is the fire going to get us?" Josh whispered.

"No!" Doug and Daniel said together. Doug started talking about how the firefighters would put the fire out, and Daniel chipped in with how it would only be a few minutes before they were off the mountain. Both of them tried hard not to look at the smoke, which was blowing towards them in ever thicker clouds. Daniel saw that Josh was crying, tears running down his cheeks.

"Hey, Josh mate, is your foot hurting?"

Josh shook his head. "'S OK," he sniffed, but it was clear that everything was not OK.

"Some end to your camping trip," Daniel said.

"Will Mabon be OK?"

"He's going to hospital, and they'll look after him." Josh was old enough not to be told more lies than necessary, but Daniel thought that the chances of Mabon being OK were slim to none.

"I don't want to move again. I want to stay with Ben. He's my best friend."

"You've moved a lot then?" Daniel asked.

"A bit. But Mum said we were going to stay in Gelli. She said Mabon had fixed it so we could all stay. It's not as good as Holyoak, but it's OK. Me and Ben have a room with bunk beds."

Daniel was desperate to ask more questions about past moves, Mel and Mabon, but interrogating an injured ten year old as he was carried off the mountain didn't seem very ethical. He steered the conversation away to more neutral territory. Josh and Ben both liked detective stories and adventure books, and like small boys everywhere, he wanted to know whether he or Doug had a gun, and what were handcuffs like and had they been in a car chase, so they struggled down the hill describing the drama of being a policeman as a way of taking Josh's mind off his troubles.

On the map, their route was shown as a path. On the ground, nothing but gorse, stones and roots. Every step had to be scouted out, and tested, before they dared to put their weight onto it. Every step downwards jarred Daniel's knees, and from his expression, Doug was suffering in the same way. The terrain was so steep that Daniel's normally well fitting running shoes were cramping his toes, and they couldn't get the relief of going down sideways or moving faster. All the time they kept talking to Josh, reassuring him that he wasn't heavy, telling each other every joke they could dredge up between them.

The air was oppressively hot and the smoke blacker and more intense. They could smell it, taste it in the backs of their throats. Their eyes were stinging, but they couldn't rub their eyes without letting go of Josh.

Daniel heard a cry from Josh, and looked over his shoulder to see a line of orange fire moving towards them, perhaps a mile away, but relentless, driven by the wind, eating the dry grass as it came. And he could hear it, a crackle, carried on the wind. Not loud, but unmistakable.

The ground got steeper. They had to zig zag to avoid near vertical slopes, getting stuck and having to go back more than once. Then there was a shout. Charlie, PC Morgan, and PC Jones were struggling up the hill towards them. Jones had stripped down to his uniform shirt, with sleeves rolled up, and his face was bright red and sweating. But Daniel noticed that Jones was the only one of the three who wasn't breathless.

"Is this a good idea Jonsey?" Doug asked, "You're looking a bit the worse for wear, mate."

"Remember that when I'm knocking you down on the rugby field," he replied, "It's a bit warm, mind. Give me some of that stuff, in fact, just give me the lad, because we're in a bit of a hurry." Jones pointed over to the west and they all saw that the orange line had moved closer. Abandoning the slings, Jones crouched on all fours and lifted Josh onto his back, being careful not to touch the injured foot. "Hold on kid, you're with the professionals now," he said. Then he grabbed one of the rucksacks and set off down the hill, sure footed and confident despite his burdens.

The others looked after him. "Appearances can be deceptive," said

153

Doug, "let's go."

Daniel heard the helicopter overhead, drowning out the noise of the fire, and the sound of the Mountain Rescue team grunting with the effort of carrying the stretcher down the hill. The helicopter hadn't come for them. A water bag dangled beneath it, waving from side to side, so that Daniel wondered how the pilot stayed in control. Then the bag opened and the leading edge of the fire blackened and died under the falling water. They weren't safe, not yet, and the stretcher-bearers were tired, even with the extra bodies to take turns. No one stumbled, no one stopped and finally they could see the stream.

The helicopter came back twice more as they half-walked, half-ran along the path back to the vehicles. The smell of burned vegetation filled the air, and now they could see the blackened earth, still smoking. Trees stood in the devastation, leaves still green, but nothing else had survived.

Chapter 18

H*e told her that none of them deserved any money. That they spied on him, made his children into spies. She was frightened. She asked what he had done.*

Charlie sat in his usual spot on the front row of the briefing. He had removed his shoes and socks and was peering at his feet with horror.

"Blisters," he said, "loads of them. I can't believe I wore these boots for *years,* pounding the streets of north Wales, and now look. Bloody mountains."

PC Morgan sniggered. "You've gone soft in CID, Charlie, mate. Who carried the lad most of the way?"

"What can I say?" asked Charlie rhetorically, "some of us are more brains than brawn," and went back to examining his blisters.

"I don't want to look at your filthy feet, Charles," said Bethan, holding her nose.

"I washed them thank you, Sarge," Charlie looked pained.

"I don't care. Put them away, and at least *try* to look professional in front of the Super."

Charlie huffed, but put his socks on. He slid his shoes under the seat. Abby sat next to him and Charlie rehearsed his tale of mountain climbing, fire and rescue, with Morgan muttering, "*he did nothing except moan,*" in the background,

"You're saying that you spent the afternoon in the fresh air, earning the thanks of grateful parents, while I was breathing in formaldehyde, and looking at a smashed skull? And telling people their son was probably dead?"

As Charlie opened his mouth to respond, Bethan poked him hard in the back. They all straightened up as Superintendent Hart walked to the front of the room with Mal. Of Daniel there was no sign. Abby wondered where he was. Kent and Owen fell out regularly, and it seemed to her that when they did, the entire station took sides, Charlie always with Owen and the Sarge always with Kent. The rows could be spectacular, but she'd seen them kissing too. It was sweet, even though they were a bit old for PDA.

Hart began, and Abby stopped speculating about her bosses and their relationship.

"Thank you all for your efforts today, and over the last few days. I'd like to keep this short and sweet because we've got another long day tomorrow. DCI Kent?"

"Thank you, ma'am." Mal began by saying that Mabon was in intensive care, still unconscious, but that the hospital was hopeful of his recovery.

"He's *serious but stable,* or one of those things doctors say when they want you to stop asking questions. He's got a broken pelvis, and a head injury. When he wakes up, we'll arrest him for abducting a child. His own child, who was in his mother's sole, court-ordered custody. Baby Dafydd is in fact Harry Bell, and he was returned to his mother today. We don't know why we were told that Harry belonged to the Edwardses." He wrote the question on the whiteboard.

"We'll also be talking to him about obstruction. Taking those two boys into the hills and terrifying their parents into not co-operating with us."

Charlie put his hand up. "Sir, when we were taking Ben off the mountain, he suggested that Mabon hadn't been all that keen on the trip. He thought Josh's mum suggested it."

PC Morgan agreed.

Mal wrote *Why did Mabon take the boys camping?* on the board. His eyes narrowed as he took in Charlie's stockinged feet, but he let it go.

"The other thing to note," said Mal, "is that Tom and Bethany Hall, and their two children, left Gelli, first thing this morning, and we think they have gone to Holyoak Hall in Devon. Harry's mother, Monica Bell, has also gone there, and it's where Mabon used to live."

"It's where Ben used to live too, sir," Charlie butted in. "He was telling us that he liked it much better there, lots more to do, and the kids went to school. He liked school." Charlie's voice implied that Ben might have made a mistake with the last item.

"DI Owen has talked to people at Holyoak, and they were glad to see the back of Mabon."

"But Mabon still has connections there," said Bethan, "Tom and Bethany, and the baby's mother. Maybe whoever DI Owen spoke to wasn't telling the whole story."

"Which would be consistent," Mal growled and wrote *Holyoak?* on the board. He went on,

"Everything we have found out about Mabon suggests that he's an unpleasant character. We know that he's changed his name multiple times, and that he told Harry's mother that he was an undercover police officer. We know that he's violent, and he's prepared to use children to frighten their parents into silence. So we have to ask ourselves whether he had a role in the deaths of the Edwards family. He'd been given permission to knock three rented houses together. He claimed that John Edwards, I quote, *shared his values,* unquote. What we don't know is what he wanted kept quiet. Was it something to do with those deaths?

157

Was he blackmailing Edwards?"

Another question went up on the board. Mal sighed and wrote *Edwards/Mabon* above his questions. Then he drew a line underneath and wrote *Jack Wall*. Hart looked round the room, and everyone realised that they ought to be copying the questions down. Clothes rustled as notebooks were pulled from pockets, and pens found.

"I'm having trouble believing that Jack Wall's death is unrelated to the deaths of the Edwards family," Mal said, "but Wall may have died by accident. Hector Lord thinks so. His body wasn't hidden by accident though, and his ghost didn't send texts and emails from his phone, so that his parents thought he was still alive. Either one of the Edwards family did it, or one of Mabon's crewage, or both."

More questions, and more scribbling.

Who hid Jack Wall's body?

Who sent the texts?

"We do know that Wall dumped his on-and-off lover, who was also his literary agent, telling her that he had fallen in love with someone else. He mentions an "*HE*" in the back of his book. Could that be Hayley Edwards? Men have killed their families because of a wife's affair. It doesn't explain Mabon's behaviour, but it could explain a lot of the rest."

"Like John Edwards found out his wife was seeing Jack Wall, got into a fight with him, Wall died, John hid the body ..." Bethan sounded as if she was warming to the story, when she was interrupted.

"... and then he waited four months to kill his family and himself? Sorry, sir, sergeant, but that won't fly." No one had heard Daniel come in to the back of the room, and they all turned to look at him. Like Charlie and the others who'd been involved in the rescue, he'd had a shower and put his clean clothes on, but Mal thought that he looked exhausted. His sleeves were rolled up and Mal could see that his arms were covered in scratches. His nose and cheekbones were blushed with sunburn and his hair was more untidy than ever. Mal recognised all the signs of Daniel about to go out on a limb, probably picking up on things that the rest of them had missed, but equally likely to be completely off the mark.

"There's another candidate for *HE*," Daniel said, "John Edwards. His family all called him Hoppy, had done since he was a kid. I rang his football club. Everyone called him Hoppy Edwards. He was arrested for gay sex, and his family are very twitchy about it. It's just as likely that he was the one having the affair."

"So why pretend Wall was still alive?" Mal asked, "And to repeat your question, why wait months to kill his family?"

"Because someone in the middle of all this is trying to be clever, but they aren't clever. It's all stuff from Midsomer Murders. Pretending people are alive when they're dead, sending the children away so their parents keep quiet."

Daniel walked to the front of the room, and held out his hand for the marker pen. "This is what I want to know," and he wrote on the board.

Who stole Hayley Edwards's clothes?

Why did John Edwards die so much later than the others?

Why did we find Harry Bell in the road?

"Why didn't the dog bark in the nighttime?" Mal asked, "Been at the Agatha Christie again?" But he said it quietly. If Hart heard, she didn't let on. Daniel mouthed *"Fuck You"* at Mal, and Hart ignored that too.

Everyone began talking at once. Bethan explained about the clothes, people exclaiming about the idea of five hundred pounds for a pair of jeans. Someone wondered loudly about Catherine Edwards, and how she was going to inherit millions, only to be reminded that she'd been in Norway when the murders happened.

Superintendent Hart cleared her throat and the room fell silent again.

"Thank you. In view of Mabon's behaviour, we have obtained a search warrant for the remaining houses on Gelli Terrace, including all the outbuildings, and Mr James Protheroe's house. Paul Jarvis will lead the search. DCI Kent will be organising interviews with the remaining residents of the commune, plus the older children — with appropriate adults. DI Owen will be visiting Holyoak Hall. Please take note of all the questions on the board, and let's see if we can answer them, ideally before the Chief Constable caves in and brings in another force to *help.*"

Hart's tone made it clear that she would regard *help* from another force as a personal affront.

When everyone else had gone she gestured to Mal and Daniel to sit down.

"Thoughts?" she asked.

"John Edwards killed his family." Mal said, sounding completely convinced, "The rest, I don't know."

"That woman I spoke to at Holyoak ... she said Mabon was a snake, a liar and a manipulator. That's what we've seen. We know he's violent. All this melodrama says Mabon to me."

"Statistically, it was John Edwards. Whether it was him having the affair, or Hayley."

And none of them could argue, because it was true, so Hart sent them home.

* * *

Daniel changed into shorts and T-shirt, and flopped down on the grass in front of the house. Mal lay down beside him and reached for his hand.

"You'll ruin those trousers."

"They need cleaning anyway."

Daniel rolled over and put his head on Mal's shoulder. He suspected that *a talk* was on the agenda, but he wanted to put it off as long as he could. He'd been ignoring calls from Megan for two days now, and she was either going to show up in person, or phone Mal. He was going to have to tell Mal about Megan leaving, and maybe Hector leaving, and about one day having kids, perhaps, and all kinds of things that he'd rather keep locked up inside and not think about.

Can't we get straight to the make-up sex?

Mal must have had the same thought. He pulled Daniel towards him and ran his hands under Daniel's T-shirt, found a nipple and squeezed, hard.

"Don't start anything you aren't going to finish, Maldwyn."

In answer, Mal put a hand on the front of Daniel's shorts, and Daniel forgot about *talking* until Mal's phone rang, and then thirty seconds later, so did his.

His call was from Hector.

"Tomorrow? I have to go to Devon tomorrow, I'll be knackered and I don't even know if I'll be back in time for dinner."

Hector begged. Daniel said he'd do his best, and that he'd tell Mal.

"Mal's here all day, busy, but here. I'll tell him he has to go."

Mal's call wasn't a short-notice dinner invitation to defend Sasha from Hector's mother. Daniel heard the words *Mrs Maddocks.* Mal stood up and took his phone call far enough away that Daniel couldn't hear any more. Daniel went into the house and started looking for things for them to eat.

"We've got to talk, haven't we?" Daniel asked when Mal came in, "I want to know what's going on, even if I'm going to hate it." He felt the tension in his body, and made himself uncross his arms and force his shoulders down from his ears.

Mal did the same. "Tell me about Hector first." He took both Daniel's hands in his, his fingers dry, and his hands so much bigger than Daniel's own. There had been times in their relationship, when being with Mal made Daniel feel safe. This wasn't one of them. This felt like standing on the edge of a cliff. A crumbling cliff.

"Hector's mother is going to Hector's for dinner tomorrow," Daniel said, "and she's bringing one of Hector's sisters-in-law, and not his favourite one. He wants us to get between them and Sasha. I said I'd do my best, but that you would definitely be there. Hector is terrified. Now who rang you?"

"Jamie Maddocks's mother. Jamie was attacked in the street last night. He's going to be OK, bruises and shock," Mal said, seeing the flare of alarm in Daniel's eyes, "Someone came, and they ran off." Mal started stroking Daniel's hands with his own.

"Was Jamie asking questions?"

"I don't know. I told him not to, but he's young and on a mission." Mal swallowed and let go of Daniel's hands to push his hair back and rub his eyes.

"There's more."

"Go on."

"I've been offered a job. In London. Setting up a task force to help kids like Ethan. Stopping them being exploited. Getting them off the streets. There would be a promotion."

Daniel felt the tears behind his eyes, but he ignored them.

"You want it."

"I want it, and I want you to come with me. To London. With your experience, you can write your own ticket. It doesn't have to be permanent."

"Why didn't you tell me before?" And then Daniel remembered. Mal had tried to tell him, and he'd said no.

"The thing is," Daniel began, and then the tears came and he couldn't stop them.

Mal held him close, stroking his hair, until Daniel pulled away and tried again.

"The thing is, Megan and Dave are taking the kids to live in Spain.

They made all the arrangements without telling me."

"And you thought that I'd done the same?"

"You did."

"All I did was arrange to see my friend Jason. He's always on at me to go back to the Met. I tried to tell you last night. I didn't expect this job. This is a dream job."

Not for me it isn't.

Daniel couldn't talk about it. Any of it. He'd told Mal about Megan, and he'd made it all about him and his job. Daniel knew he was being unfair, but he couldn't help himself. He wanted to talk about Andy Carter, but the words wouldn't come. He sat and looked at his hands, and held the tears back.

"Dan, I know there's more. Tell me."

Daniel shook his head. His lips were stuck together, and his jaw tight. He couldn't speak.

"That's not like Megan," Mal said, "is that why you felt so sad about little Harry? Losing him as well as your nephew and niece?"

Daniel felt the waves of sorrow wash over him — Andy Carter, Megan, Harry, the Edwards children.

"Can I borrow your car?" he said, "I want to go to Devon tonight. Then I can be back for Hector's dinner party."

"I thought you were taking a driver?"

"If I go tonight, I won't need one. Please Mal."

"Where are you going to sleep?"

"I. Don't. Know. Are you going to lend me your car, or shall I take the unmarked?" The unmarked car in question was kept at the police station for anyone whose car broke down. It was roadworthy and clean, but that was all that could be said about it. Mal knew as well as Daniel did, that the car would be hell on a long journey.

"Text me when you get there, and if you stop for a sleep. Please don't make me worry."

163

"I won't."

Daniel went upstairs for clean clothes to take with him. When he came back, Mal had made him a travel mug of coffee and raided the chocolate stash. He hugged Daniel very hard. "Be careful, love," he said.

Daniel pulled away, gathered up his things and left. He didn't look back.

Chapter 19

He told her to look upstairs. She screamed. He said that they were safe now. He said his wife was safe too.

Daniel drove north to pick up the motorway. Night had started to fall, and as he turned south onto the M6, the cloudless sky was inky. Traffic was light, and Daniel fell into a rhythm — indicate, pull out, overtake, indicate, pull back in, taking a sip of the coffee when the road in front was empty. He let the stereo play randomly from his playlist until *Don't Leave me This Way* followed *Small Town Boy* and tears started running down his face. He jabbed the off switch, and then put it back on again, and the two songs on repeat, letting his mind drift into sadness.

When he came to a set of roadworks, he slowed down, and ate some of the chocolate with the last of the coffee. That Mal had made him the coffee, had looked after him, made him sadder. South of Birmingham, and safely on the M5, his speed crept up, unnoticed, until he was doing over 100, and the sight of a blue flashing light in the far distance jerked him back to his senses, and the speed limit.

He was driving too fast, listening to music that made him cry, feeling sorry for himself and not caring. He wanted to talk to Mal, to talk about Megan without getting upset, to try to make Mal *explain* about why London was so important, but every time he tried, his lips sealed themselves together. Because what he *needed* to say was that when his eyes closed he saw Andy Carter, in pain, moaning with pain, that he, Daniel, had inflicted. Andy Carter had died. And Daniel couldn't get past it. He knew that he needed help, that he couldn't deal with it on his own. Before this week, he would have told Megan, but Megan had changed everything between them.

Mal would understand, if he could find a way to say the words. They kissed, and fucked, and cuddled, and went running and swimming, and to the pub, and it was all great. When they did talk, it was fine. It would be fine, if he could unfreeze enough to get the words out. *I think I am going mad. I can't forget what happened to Andy Carter. I can't forget that night and how frightened I was. It won't go away. I need help.*

Four hours into the drive he started to feel tired. He'd crossed the border into Devon and he needed to look again at his directions to find Holyoak, so he thought that he may as well try to get some sleep. He pulled into a service station and parked amongst the trucks, a few lights flickering in cabs as the drivers settled down for the night. Daniel smiled to himself, remembering his teenage fantasies about sexy truck drivers. He got his blanket from the back of the car, and let the passenger seat down flat. He kept his promise to Mal and sent a text and got a *love you, x,* in return. The motorway hummed in the background, drivers turned their engines on and off, and there were shouts as travellers went in and out of the cafe and shops. He let the noises fill his mind, and although it was the last thing he expected, he went to sleep.

* * *

166

Mal was beginning to think that Cai Jones was the most irritating person he'd met in his police career. He'd pulled drunks out of gutters, been assaulted by extremists from both right and left, and by his own colleagues intent on a cover up. He'd been shot. Daniel knew how to push all his buttons and could reduce him to incoherent rage in seconds. He had sat in more *No Comment* interviews than he could count. But for sheer under-the-skin unpleasantness Cai was going to be hard to beat.

If Cai had taken the *No Comment* route, Mal would have dealt with it. Instead Cai answered every question with a barbed dig at him, the investigation and Clwyd Police in general. They'd disturbed the hippies at breakfast, with their search warrant, suggesting that perhaps one of the adults might like to take the children out, so they didn't get upset. Cai said *No way*, the children may as well learn what the police were like, sooner rather than later.

"We wouldn't want them to grow up thinking that they could trust you to help them," he said.

Mel told him to stop being an arse, and she and Becca took the children down to the river. Cai followed them round, flitting from room to room, wondering aloud if they were hoping to find a stash of porn, or had brought drugs to plant, and were they getting off on looking through women's underwear.

"Of course we don't have much," he said, "We share. It's an alien concept for people like you, but if you practised, you might be able to understand."

Cai had the ability to be constantly in the way, standing between the CSIs and whatever it was they were trying to look at, or being just behind someone as they stepped backwards. Paul Jarvis had to go outside and beg a cigarette from the PC on duty, despite having quit twenty years before.

The search of the house produced little of interest. Cai was right in that none of them had much stuff. There were plenty of books, and games, and children's toys, but few clothes, or gadgets. The only drugs were herbal remedies, and a few paracetamol. The only alcohol was home made cider. A larder cupboard held jams, chutneys, pickles, and jars of sauerkraut and passata. The chest freezer was full of their own produce, and there were stores of apples and root vegetables. They looked at it all, accompanied by patronising lectures from Cai. The loft space held empty suitcases, and camping equipment. Outdoor coats and boots were in a porch by the back door. Two computers were kept in their own room.

"We're not luddites, we just don't want screen addiction for our kids," Cai said, staring rudely at one of the CSIs who was looking at his phone. "We use the technology, but we're not enslaved by it, unable to function without a screen in every pocket." He still protested against the computers being loaded into the police van.

"Thank goodness you aren't enslaved by it," muttered Paul Jarvis, not very quietly, "you won't miss it at all."

Of Hayley Edwards's missing clothes, they could find no sign. Tom and Bethany's room had been stripped of everything but the furniture. It didn't look as though they would be coming back, or as Cai put it,

"Well done, you've managed to drive them away, you must be pleased at disrupting the lives of innocent children."

"Our lads carried your boy off the mountain yesterday, mate," one of the uniformed officers began, but a warning look from Mal shut him up.

If Cai expected that he could irritate the searchers into sloppiness, he failed. He made them more determined, and in the toolshed they found two mobile phones, wrapped in a plastic bag. Both were new and top of the range, so without the passcodes they were going to be difficult to access. But they matched the paperwork in the Edwards's house, and Mal had no doubt whose they were. Cai denied all knowledge of them.

By lunchtime every floorboard and wall had been examined, every drawer opened, every shelf emptied and every mattress tipped. There was no more that they could do.

Mal arranged transport for them all to the police station, "where you will be interviewed under caution." Cai sneered. Mal thought of the CID team patiently assembling details of each of their lives, and wished that he'd arrested the lot of them on day one.

* * *

Daniel dreamed that he was in a sauna, dripping with sweat, as Andy Carter poured more water onto the hot rocks. A shadowy figure stepped forward with a gun. Daniel lurched toward Andy, shouting "No!" and woke with a start, cracking his hand on something sharp. The car windows were steamed up, sunlight heating the interior to tropical temperatures. He wiped a porthole in the condensation and saw that the lorry park had emptied while he slept. He had been oblivious to the noise of them leaving, and despite the cramped space, and oppressive humidity, his head was clear, as if the tide of misery had gone out, leaving the sand clean and fresh.

He was beginning to see his way through the mess and confusion of the case, to understand who must have killed the Edwards family, and why Jack Wall's body had been hidden. His anger at the way Harry and the other children had been treated was growing. Seren and Stella had been murdered, and if he was right, there was no chance of getting justice for them. He saw the row of dominoes, all standing on their ends. Harry, Seren, Stella, Hayley, John, Jack, Monica, the hippies all in a line. A single push and they all started to fall, one after another. The real tragedy, he thought, was that none of it was *meant*.

His personal problems were going to have to wait. He needed to tell his sister how he felt about her behaviour. He needed to talk rationally to Mal about the future, and somehow he needed to get beyond Andy Carter's death. He opened a suitcase in his mind, put the problems inside and closed it up. Labelled it: *Not needed on voyage.* It was time to find Holyoak Hall.

His directions took him down a narrow lane, hedges almost touching overhead, over a cattle grid and into an informal car park, next to the side of a substantial stone built house. A portico covered the front door, which stood open, revealing a stone flagged floor and walls lined with battered panelling. Inside it looked dark and cool, but he ignored it in favour of the dappled sunlight outside, and the sound of children shouting, contrasting with quieter adult voices. He walked round to the front of the house, and gasped. It was beautiful, and he understood why it drew people back.

French doors stood open onto a wide terrace. The house behind was covered in wisteria, swags of purple flowers hanging over most of the windows. He guessed it was Victorian, though the gothic was restrained. Below the terrace, what should have been a lawn had been allowed to become a wild meadow, overgrown with soft-headed grasses, buttercups, dandelion clocks, and every colour of wild flower. The meadow seemed to be full of children — playing frisbee, practicing cartwheels and making daisy chains. In reality there were no more than six or seven of them, and as soon as a wasp appeared, or someone tripped, the idyll would break, but for now he smiled with delight.

On the terrace itself, a group of people sat around a big table, drinking coffee, and eating toast. Daniel recognised Tom and Bethany, and as he stepped forward to introduce himself, they recognised him, and their faces fell. He wished that he wasn't always the disturber of the peace, the asker of intrusive questions, that he could simply sit down and enjoy the morning.

Then a dark haired figure came out of the darkness of the house, through the French doors into the sunshine, and there was a shout, "Man!"

"Do you want a cuddle?" Monica asked, and he lifted a wriggling, laughing Harry into his arms.

"Hi," he said, happiness filling his body as he felt the little boy, solid and well-made, and desperate to go and play in the meadow with the others

"Can he go down to the meadow?" Daniel asked Monica and she said, "Try and stop him." Even so, Daniel carried Harry down the stone steps and put him down on the grass. Harry looked round for Monica, who had poured two mugs of coffee and brought them over to the steps.

"He doesn't like me to be out of sight," she said, "so do you mind if we sit here? I'm guessing you have questions."

Daniel said that he did, and that he had questions for Tom and Bethany and probably for Jay Grieve too.

"I want to ask you about Mabon," Daniel said, "which might be painful. I get that, but it would really help."

Monica folded her arms across her chest, "Sure. I've talked to everyone else about him, why not you?" Harry came running up, and threw himself at his mother. She lifted him up for a kiss and he immediately wriggled free, running off shouting. "This is how he's been," she said, "keeps coming to check in, then he's off. Caitlin has started bossing him around." Daniel had to think who Caitlin was.

"Tom and Bethany's daughter?"

These people all know each other. They must have recognised Harry. They kept a tiny child away from his mother and they're sitting having breakfast as if nothing is wrong.

* * *

A call to Veronica produced a childcare worker who could entertain the little children at the social services Contact Centre. Cai — inevitably — complained loudly and longwindedly, until his solicitor arrived. At that point, several things became much clearer to Mal.

The first thing was that Cai's belligerence came from a place of privilege. The solicitor was a sharp-suited young woman, from a London firm, who had obviously dealt with Cai before. He must have called her in the morning, while they were searching the house. Bethan confirmed that Cai and Becca both came from professional families, and the solicitor worked in Cai's family firm, which had branches all around the UK.

The second thing was that Cai wasn't all bad. The solicitor's time wasn't cheap, but he insisted that she attend all the interviews, including Mel's. Mal thought that was because Cai wouldn't be picking up the bill, but Bethan put him right, saying that she'd overheard — quite legitimately, the conversation was in reception — Cai saying that he'd pay for her time, no matter how long it all took. He wasn't promising that the time would be paid for, Bethan emphasised, he was promising to pay the bills himself.

Finally, and this took a bit longer to work out, Cai was in love with Mabon. Not necessarily in a sexual way, but he'd been seduced into activism and housing co-ops by Mabon. Cai was almost frantic with worry about Mabon's injuries, and Mal realised that his bad temper was at least in part, a way of relieving the tension.

None of this knowledge made the interview any easier, or Cai any less irritating. Nor did it produce much helpful information.

The afternoon was an exercise in frustration and contradiction.

Cai said that he had met Mabon at a protest against the destruction of an ancient woodland. He described Mabon standing on a bulldozer, stopping it moving, and speaking with passion about humanity's need for trees.

"He pointed at this oak," Cai said, pointing, with his own hand, as if seeing Mabon standing in front of him, "and told us the events in our history that it had witnessed. It was two hundred years old, and they were going to kill it, to build some shitty railway line that no one wants. He had us all in tears, even the bulldozer driver." Then Cai's face closed up, and he said, "The police came, and dragged him away." Mabon as the tragic hero, thought Mal cynically.

He was right about the tree though.

Mel said that she had met both Mabon and Cai at Holyoak Hall. Cai said that he had never been to Holyoak, Becca said they knew lots of the residents and stayed there more than once. Mal couldn't tell whether any of them believed anything that they were saying.

Cai said that Harry was Mabon's son, and that Monica was telling lies to keep Mabon from seeing him.

"She threatened to take the boy to live in Italy with her relatives. Mabon would never see him again."

"Monica has a court order giving her sole custody. Mabon can see Harry at a contact centre." Bethan said, pushed beyond her usual patience.

"It's all lies. I've lived with Mabon for years. He isn't violent. A father should be able to see his son."

Mel agreed that Mabon was a good father, and that if Monica had been reasonable, no abduction would have been necessary. When Mal suggested that Monica must have been devastated by Harry's kidnapping, Mel laughed bitterly.

"She could have one of mine. She could have them all. Let her see what it's like bringing them up on her own."

Mel and Becca both denied that they knew John Edwards owned all the houses in Gelli Terrace. Cai said they all knew, and that John Edwards and Mabon were discussing John handing them over to their tenants, and that they all knew that, too.

They agreed in three things — none of them had heard any shots on the night of the killings, none of them knew Jack was having an affair, and none of them knew Jack was dead. Mal was certain that they were all lying, and the other detectives agreed with him.

Then they had to talk to the boys.

Chapter 20

S he was shaking and crying. He wanted to slap her, slap all of them *in their dirty clothes and their grasping minds. Pretending to be his* *friend. Betraying him.*

"I didn't realise that you knew Tom and Bethany," said Daniel. Monica flushed, her cheeks slashed with red.

"Yes, well." she said, folding her arms again, "I didn't know they'd be here."

"They knew where Harry was, and didn't tell you."

"They believed Mark — Mabon. Everyone always does. I don't blame them, not really." But her body said differently.

Daniel asked her to tell him about Mabon, about their relationship. He wasn't certain about the timeline, but there seemed to be some crossover between Mabon-and-Mel, and Mark-and-Monica.

"You're right,"Monica said, when Daniel suggested it, "He came to visit, and I thought he was cute and one thing led to another. I knew about Mel, and the other housing co-op, but he gave me the undercover cop story, and said that I was seeing the real him. Then I got pregnant, and he was over the moon, only he kept going away."

Mabon disappeared for weeks, then came back, was attentive and kind for a few days, then disappeared again. Monica started to suspect that Mel wasn't the only one being lied to, and a conversation with people from Holyoak confirmed her fears.

"Lather, rinse and repeat," said Monica, "everyone says don't blame yourself, he was such a good liar, blah, blah."

Harry's birth certificate made no mention of his father, but Monica said Mabon started bullying her for shared custody.

"I got so lucky," she said, "a law student from the university helped me, they run a free clinic, and we got the court order. I said he could see Harry under supervision, but not at my house. I didn't want him there, not after I found out that he was lying about everything."

Mabon had covered his tracks well, changing his name, never telling Monica where his other home was, relying on his undercover cop story. Even when that had failed, Monica never knew where he lived. Four hours drive away, and no one had found them, Daniel thought. The police would have looked, especially after Monica had been assaulted.

"It wasn't your fault," Daniel said, "and I don't think he'll try the same trick again."

"I'm moving to Italy," she said, "I've got family there, and I can get a job." Her cheeks flushed red again, and she looked up at the party on the terrace. "Everyone here says they're sorry, but, you know what? I don't care any more."

"We'd like to see him charged with abduction," said Daniel, "so let us know where you are. For the trial."

"I don't care about that either. I want a new start, where no one knows anything about me."

Daniel squeezed her hand. "Do what you need to do," he said, and Harry chose that moment to come and 'check in' with a leap onto his mother's lap.

"Man," he said, pointing at Daniel, "bye."

Monica leaned over, holding onto Harry, and kissed Daniel's cheek.

"He likes you really," she said, "and he's decided that he likes your bear better than his old one."

Daniel ruffled Harry's hair and stood up. Time to see what Tom and Bethany had to say for themselves.

* * *

They are all so unhappy. Seeking the good life and finding only despair.

Mal could have cried for them all, if he had any sympathy left after finding the bodies of the Edwards family. *Poor little rich kids.* He probably wasn't being fair, but five people were dead, and whatever three of them had done, two of them had done nothing, and their deaths would always be unforgivable. He needed desperately to talk it all over with Daniel, but Daniel was on his way back from Devon, and then they were promised to Hector. So he found Bethan and Charlie and asked what they thought.

"Weird. All three of them. Weird." Charlie's take was typical Charlie.

"Could you expand on that, do you think?" Mal asked, and Charlie demonstrated how he'd made it into CID.

"I've been reading about *intentional communities* and they attract a lot of professional types, with plenty of money. People who could have all the things you are supposed to want, but that don't make you happy — though a nice car and a fifty-four inch flat screen TV would do a lot for my happiness, gotta be honest."

"And?"

"And reading between the lines, they also attract people who are vulnerable. Like they've just got divorced, or they've had a breakdown. People like Mel who want help looking after the kids. Or people like John Edwards who was hiding from the world. So kind of a perfect hunting ground for Mabon. Because it seems to me that what he wanted was an audience, fans, worshippers."

Bethan was nodding. "That's exactly it," she said, "Mabon saw himself as leader of a cult, with Cai as his acolyte. I've been wondering whether Mabon wasn't kidnapping the boys to keep the others in order at all, whether the others wanted Mabon out of the way to protect *him*."

"Protect him from what?"

"From us, from what we might find out. I'm starting to wonder if Mabon had a hand in killing the Edwardses, or Jack Wall …"

Charlie interrupted, "… or he knows who did it and he was blackmailing them …"

"They all know who did it." Bethan folded her arms, "They aren't going to tell us. We need some decent forensics. Or a witness."

No. We need Daniel, who will see the pattern in this mess.

* * *

Tom and Bethany didn't want to talk to Daniel.

"You need to understand," he said, "that I have the right to arrest you both for perverting the course of justice, and at a stretch, abduction of a child. My colleagues from Exeter will be more than happy to take you to their police station. Perhaps they will tell you about the time they have been wasting trying to find Harry Bell. Charges are almost guaranteed. While you're there, you can spend some time thinking about how Monica has been feeling for the last few months. You can wonder whether Caitlin and Myfannwy are being well cared for without you." It was cruel, but what they had done to Harry and Monica had been cruel.

Bethany burst into tears. Tom said, "We didn't know."

"You did know," said Daniel, "you knew that the little boy Mabon brought to Gelli was his son Harry. You knew that he had no intention of letting him see his mother again, even changing his name."

"We didn't know he'd abducted him."

"Oh stop lying." Daniel felt his grasp on reason sliding. He was on the point of grabbing Tom by his shirt and shaking him. "Stop lying. You've all lied and lied. Five people are *dead*. A court gave custody of Harry to *Monica*. Mabon *put her in hospital.* Your lies aren't going to change any of it."

Bethany sobbed harder, rocking forwards and backwards on the bench, holding her hands over her face.

"Why can't you leave us alone?" Tom rubbed Bethany's back and stroked her hair.

"Tom, listen to me. You knew about Harry, and we can prove it. Harry is back where he belongs, the boys are with their parents. But those two little girls are dead. I want justice for them. Don't you care?"

Bethany looked up, her face red, and soggy with tears. "Of course we care. We loved those girls."

"Then tell me the truth. Answer my questions."

"And if we do, you won't arrest us?"

"Not about Harry, not today." That was the only promise he could make, but Tom nodded.

"OK."

* * *

Mal took the call from Jason Maclean in his office with the door closed.

"You weren't kidding that Glamorgan don't want you back. Like a dog with a bone, seemed to be the consensus. Which I was always told was a good trait for a police officer, but maybe not in Wales?"

"Not when the dog is after one of them. I'm not sure it's a particularly Welsh problem."

Jason agreed.

"Anyway, I got the *one bad apple* runaround. Even the woman you told me about — Stamford-Wallis — didn't want to know about any more cases, and she was on your side. You need to convince that Jamie lad to keep out of it."

If only.

"The good news is that there is a lot of interest in having a look at young queer kids washing up in our fair city. There are charities, and social services, for the victims, but no one to clean up the pimps and the other vultures. It's a box ticking exercise, sure it is, but you could do some good as well as make brownie points for the Commissioner."

"I told you why I can't come."

"And I told you that the boyfriend could come too. They'd be fighting over him."

"I'll talk to him, Jase, but don't hold your breath."

Mal couldn't imagine Daniel away from north Wales, stuck in the city, with all the people and dirt, not knowing anyone. Which didn't mean he wasn't going to try to persuade him. In the meantime, he had a hospital visit to make.

* * *

One of the residents of Holyoak Hall appeared with a tray of coffee and cake, put it down in front of them and disappeared again. Neither Bethany's crying fit, nor the presence of an angry policeman ruffled the surface of the sunny morning. The children carried on playing in the meadow, the adults sat and watched, coffee in hand, soaking up the scene and the sunshine.

Worthy was a good description of the cake, which seemed to have been made without sugar, butter or eggs, but he ate it anyway, not knowing when he would get the chance to eat again. Happily the cake-maker was not in charge of coffee procurement.

"I'd like to ask you about the night that the Edwardses were killed," he began. Bethany started crying again, and Tom put his arm round her shoulders.

"It's been terrible," Tom said, "we saw them every day, then, bam, gone."

"There were shots," said Daniel, "two in the night, and one in the early morning. They would have been loud."

"We heard them. I couldn't say the exact time. The baby doesn't sleep well yet, so we're always up and down. But we didn't know they were next door, we really didn't. There is shooting, not often, but enough. Farmers, poachers."

"When we asked you all the next day, you said that you hadn't heard anything. Why?"

"Mabon said we hadn't, so we agreed." As if it were the most normal thing in the world.

"That's what you usually did, follow Mabon's lead? Even when you knew it was a lie?"

Tom had to think about that one. Daniel saw the wheels turning. He suspected that Tom's automatic response would be another lie and wondered whether he would be able to resist. To Daniel's surprise, he did. Tom breathed out, his body slumping in defeat. He held out the hand that wasn't stroking Bethany's back.

"You're the police, right. We've all been arrested at protests and stuff. As soon as you look on your computer, our names come up. We live communally, homeschool our kids, grow our own food ..." Tom trailed off.

"You thought that we wouldn't treat you as well as someone who lived in a house with a mortgage, and a regular job?"

"A reasonable expectation, based on experience."

"Environmental protests, possible murder, assault, child abduction.

One of these things is not like the others. I can understand that you might be wary. What I need to understand is why you followed Mabon's lead about Jack Wall, about Harry, about his disappearance with Josh and Ben."

The colour drained from Tom's face.

"You knew that Jack Wall was dead."

Tom whispered "Yes."

"You knew that his body was hidden in his house, and you pretended he was still alive."

Another whispered "Yes."

"Why? Why would you do that? Our pathologist thinks Jack's death might have been an accident. So why cover it up?"

Tears started to roll down Tom's cheeks, and he wiped them away. "It was horrible. It's been horrible for months. That's not who we are, Bethany and me. We want what's best for our kids, for the planet. Mabon ..." Tom wiped his face again and leaned forward. "You probably think that places like this," gesturing with his arm at the beauty around them, "are meant for people like us. They're not. We can come and volunteer, but if we want to stay permanently, we'd have to buy shares, and we can't afford it. Everywhere else is the same. You'd think dropping out of the rat race would be cheap." Tom shook his head. "It is until you've got kids. We can't live in a squat with two kids, and Myfannwy doesn't sleep so we're always tired. We don't want to keep moving."

"And Mabon told you that you could stay in Gelli, as long as you did what he said?"

"We thought we'd found our forever home."

Daniel almost felt sorry for them. But then he thought about Harry and Monica.

"Did you bring anything from Gelli that wasn't yours?" he asked, "some clothes?"

"How did you know?"

* * *

Mabon had not woken up. The smell of smoke still clung to his body, though he was wearing nothing but a sheet and a lot of bandages. Mal was allowed into the Intensive Care bay for long enough to introduce himself to the two people by Mabon's bedside, and to ask them to talk to him. They asked for five more minutes.

"The longer he's unconscious, the less likely he is to wake up. His brain took one hell of a knock." The nurse taking care of Mabon didn't sound hopeful. "People are in this ward because they're very ill. We're doing our best." She showed him into a room behind the nurses' station, where he could talk to Mabon's parents.

It was nearer twenty minutes before they joined him. Mal couldn't judge how old they were — they could have been anywhere between fifty and eighty — and they looked as if life had been battering them down for a long time.

"I'm sorry to meet you in these circumstances," he said, "and I'm also sorry to say that I don't know your names ..."

"Dixon, Paul and Mary Dixon. Our son's name is Marcus." Paul Dixon gave a twisted smile. "I'm sure you know him by some other name, or maybe several other names. Ask your questions. It won't be the first time we've spoken to the police."

Mal wanted to know about Mabon, but he also wanted to know about these two.

"We're both doctors, GPs in Bangor. Marcus is our only child."

The story came out slowly. The rebellious teenager, who ran away from home to join a group of squatters, and then an anarchist collective. Then arrests for environmental protests, criminal damage, breach of

183

the peace, moves to different intentional communities.

"He used to come back when he needed to recharge his batteries, or because he needed us to fund a defence lawyer."

"He rings though, every few weeks, that's how the hospital found us — Mum and Dad in his phone." said Mary Dixon, "Wek new he'd moved back to Wales, though not exactly where."

"We knew we had a grandchild, but we've only seen photographs. Marcus did say he'd bring the boy — Dafydd — but he never did."

"Why the name changes?" Mal asked, wondering whether Monica would let these two gentle people meet Harry.

"He didn't approve of us. He talked all sorts of nonsense about modern medicine, as if he could cure cancer with a few herbs. We argued. So he changed his name the first time to spite us. Then I think it became a habit. He'd move to somewhere new and change his name."

"We stopped arguing," said Mary, "but I did ask him about his name once. He said he'd never liked the name Marcus. But that doesn't explain all the others."

"Every name had a different story behind it. Like calling himself Mabon because he moved to Wales. He's as Welsh as you, Chief Inspector, he didn't need a new name. It was all made up. I don't think even he knew who he was in the end."

Chapter 21

You need better things, you want better things? He opened the wardrobes and threw clothes at her. The clothes his wife had bought with his money and worn to seduce another man. He told her to take them. All of them.

Daniel was exhausted. He had stopped twice on the way back from Devon, for coffee and sugar, and apples to eat when the traffic slowed down. It slowed down often, unlike in the middle of the night. He wanted a long shower, and to fall asleep in Mal's arms. Making small talk with Hector's mother was not on his wish list for the evening. But Hector would do it for him, and Sasha needed their help, so, no choice.

Mal had coffee waiting, clean, ironed jeans and shirt for him to put on after the shower, and offered to come into the shower and wash his back.

"We know how that would end, *Cariad,* and then I would fall asleep in a post orgasmic haze. Which you would have to explain to Hector. Talk to me about the hippies instead."

Mal poured some coffee into one of the rainbow mugs they'd got from the fair trade shop.

"They told more lies, contradicted each other, and confused themselves as well as us. They deny hearing the shots, they deny knowing that Jack Wall was dead, or that he was having an affair. The most interesting thing is that Cai produced a very sharp solicitor, and paid for her to represent Mel as well as him and Becca. It turns out that Cai is from a family of lawyers."

That made sense to Daniel. In his experience, the people with the self confidence to bait the police in the way that Cai did were either career criminals or came from privilege. He didn't think Cai was a career criminal. But he'd been wrong before. He drank some coffee and refilled his cup.

"What did the boys have to say?"

"Now that was *very* interesting."

They'd seen Ben first, in their soft interview room; he and Bethan, Ben, the solicitor and Cai. Mal had been concerned that Ben wouldn't want to talk in front of his dad, but he was fine. Calm and confident, with none of his father's aggression or bad temper. When they discussed it afterwards, neither Mal nor Bethan had any sense that he'd been told what to say.

"Talking to Ben made me think better of Cai, to be honest," Mal told Daniel, "Because he came across as such a nice lad. Open, friendly, thoughtful. He said that he liked sharing a room with Josh, but wished they could have stayed at Holyoak. He and Josh got on well with Seren Edwards. He thought Mabon was OK."

"What about the camping trip?"

"He wondered if it was to cheer them up after Seren died, because they'd been good friends."

"Yeah right,"

"That's what I thought, but Ben said it was the sort of thing the adults would do, and he sounded as if he believed it. No, the most interesting things he said were about Josh. He said that Josh was *nosy*, and there weren't so many *spying* places at Gelli as there were at Holyoak. Ben implied that Josh liked to eavesdrop, and when I asked him why, he said he thought Josh worried about his mother, so he liked to find out what the adults were saying. He didn't like surprises."

Ben had cried about Seren's death, and the deaths of all the Edwards family. He talked about playing with Seren, and taking Betsy the dog into the woods, and then sobbed, as if remembering the dog was the last straw. Cai had held his son, looking daggers at Mal and Bethan, clearly holding them responsible for Ben's distress. But when he opened his mouth to say so, the solicitor put a warning hand on his arm, and he stopped. They'd let Ben go then, both close to tears themselves.

"It's like we've been banging heads with the adults for so long that we forgot how the children must be feeling."

"Have we been played? By the grown-up hippies I mean?"

Mal said he'd been wondering the same. "We should have had them in before. Treated them as suspects from day one. My fault. Except every time I think I've got them nailed as bullshitters, I think maybe they really are trying to live better lives."

Daniel put his arms round Mal and kissed his ear. "This is why I love you," he said, "you *think.*"

Mal kissed him back, until the post orgasmic haze became a probability, and then reality. They showered together — to save time — and ran, giggling, down to the car.

"Was that make-up sex without an argument first?" Daniel asked.

"We can have sex without an argument. Don't argue with me all evening, and I'll prove it."

Daniel rested his hand on Mal's knee, pleased beyond measure not to be driving. The car windows were open, and the evening scents came in as they drove through the lanes. The denim shirt felt soft against Daniel's skin, his feet cool in Birkenstocks, his hair damp from the shower, and the post-orgasmic haze buzzing gently. They would have a good meal, help out a friend, and then he got to go home with Mal, who was looking even sexier than usual. When the suitcase he'd packed away in the morning tried to pry itself open, he piled weights on top of it.

Later. I'll open the suitcases later. Not tonight.

* * *

Lady Belinda Ashleigh Lord lived by the words that *you can't be too rich or too thin.* She had been a slim and elegant young woman, and she was a slim and elegant middle-aged woman now. Ginny, Hector thought, was just thin. She wore the same clothes as his mother, but they never made her look elegant, just dull. His mother's complexion suited white, and beige and pale pastels. Ginny needed colour. But Ginny would be Lady Virginia one day, and she was modelling herself on the current title-holder.

He'd told his mother that no one would be dressing up. Her version of not dressing up involved white linen trousers, and what Hector thought of as a silk vest, with a wisp of cardigan over it. A pale blue scarf, almost exactly the colour of her eyes, draped around her neck as if held by static electricity. Her high-heeled wedge sandals matched the scarf, as did her earrings. She looked as if the slightest breeze would blow her away, and she smelled of spring flowers. Hector always felt like a cart horse next to a thoroughbred when he saw her. He almost felt sorry for Ginny, who lived daily with all this effortless feminine perfection, but then Ginny looked down her nose at his cottage, and he went back to wondering why his brother had married her.

"Darling!" Hector's mother cried and crushed her cart horse of a son against her tiny self. Her tiny self who swam, and ran, and rode every day, competing in Point-to-Point races every winter, and the

188

village cross country race *just for a laugh.* She could slaughter grouse and pheasants with the best of them. If things had been different, he often thought, she would have been a formidable athlete. But things weren't different.

"Mother," he said, "this is Sasha, and her daughter Arwen. Arwen, Sasha, my mother, *Belinda.*"

"*Lady Belinda,*" Ginny muttered. Hector ignored her. "And this is my brother Hilary's wife, Ginny," Ginny extended a limp hand.

For once, his mother did exactly the right thing. She dropped into a crouch and held out a hand to Arwen. "Good evening, Arwen," she said, "that's a fairy name. Do you like fairies?"

"It's an elf name, but there are fairies in the garden. Are there fairies in your garden?"

"Of course." She looked up at Sasha. "I always wanted a girl. One as clever and pretty as Arwen." She looked back at Arwen, "Would you show me where the fairies are, my dear?"

Arwen reached happily for her hand and pulled her towards the laurels.

* * *

"So what did Josh have to say? And how's his foot?"

"Not broken. It's all strapped up, in one of those Velcro boot things, and he's using crutches for a few days."

Josh hadn't been calm and confident. He'd wriggled in his seat, rubbed his hands on his jeans and up and down his sleeves. Every time Mel tried to catch his eye, he looked away. She seemed as if she was having to make great efforts not to tell him off, or pull his hands away from the constant rubbing, or tell him what to say. They'd asked Josh the same questions as they'd asked Ben, about how he liked living in

Gelli, about the Edwards family, and about the camping trip.

"He was upset about Seren, about all of them, but especially Seren. But he was anxious too. He said Seren was worried about her dad. He wanted to know what depression was, because that's what Seren said her dad had, and could you die of it? Seren told him that his mum and dad argued all the time. And *then* he said that Seren's mum used to go and see Jack, and maybe that's why they argued."

Mel had interrupted. "He's making it up."

"No, Mum, I'm not. I saw them kissing. I *did.* That's why grown ups argue. I'm not stupid."

Mel looked like she was ready to drag her son away, but the solicitor gave her a *calm down* look.

"He does make things up." Mel had folded her arms and stared into the corner of the room.

That's when Josh had looked like crying. "I *don't.* You said we weren't going to move again, and then ..."

Mel looked at her son with hard eyes and he stopped talking. After that he'd said almost nothing. The camping trip had been "fine," Mabon was "nice."

"He knows something, and he wants to tell us, but he's too frightened of what his mother will do."

The pieces of the case began to rearrange themselves in Daniel's mind. What Tom had said about not being able to afford to live the alternative life, Cai's privileged background, the millions that John Edwards controlled, the camping trip.

"Was the camping trip about keeping *Josh* out of the way?"

But Mal didn't get chance to answer, because they were there, and it was time to stop being policemen and start being friends. Mal parked and they walked round to Hector's garden, towards the sound of Sasha's voice.

* * *

"That sounds like the fairies arriving now," said Sasha. Hector snorted, and Ginny looked confused.

"I've invited two of our friends," he said, "they're gay."

Ginny looked horrified. Whether at the reference to gay men as fairies, or at the thought of their joining the party wasn't clear. Mal and Daniel must have heard the voices, because they came round the corner into the garden, and Ginny's eyes widened in surprise. Hector had to clear his throat to stop her staring at Mal, who was looking gorgeous in black jeans and a black linen shirt, and even black espadrilles. He had his arm round Daniel, who looked very tired, in soft blue jeans and shirt, hair sticking up. Daniel had big hugs for Sasha and Hector, and a gentle handshake for Ginny.

"Where's Arwen?" Daniel asked, and was dragged down to the end of the garden by Hector while Sasha went to look at the dinner — "Caterers, and loads of wine in case it's horrible". Ginny looked appalled, so Mal was left to turn the charm on.

"Talk to my mother about plants," Hector whispered, but he didn't get the chance. Arwen babbled about fairies and Belinda appeared enchanted.

"Hector, darling, it's not that I have ever been disappointed in you, but I did so long for a little girl."

Hector suggested that there would be grandchildren. "Oh, but we need boys first, so it will be *ages* before I get any little girls." Because of course, the sex of grandchildren would shape themselves to Belinda's needs.

"I'm hoping that you will see more of Arwen," Hector said.

"I do hope so too. *Such* a delightful child. A credit to her mother."

"I think so," he said.

191

The dinner was delicious. To Ginny's obvious disapproval, Arwen joined them for the first course — poached salmon tartlets — and then went willingly to bed. Hector wondered how far Sasha had had to walk her to achieve that effect, given the distraction of new and exciting visitors. Without Arwen and Sasha, Hector needed conversation, so he asked about Devon.

"It's a long way from north Wales," said Daniel, "but it was a useful trip. I think we're making progress."

"What is it you do?" Ginny asked without any apparent interest in the answer.

"Coppers," said Sasha coming in and closing the door very gently so as not to wake the sleeping Arwen, "grisly murders a speciality. Of course they'd be lost without an exceptional pathologist to point them in the right direction." She ruffled Hector's hair, and went into the kitchen for the next course. Hector jumped up and collected their used plates.

"Detectives, how *exciting*," said Belinda, "What are you working on now?"

Mal said that they might have heard of the case. Ginny had but Belinda said she never watched the news. *Too depressing don't you think?*

"But I *love* detective stories. Dorothy Sayers, Anthea Fraser, and my very favourite, Marjorie Allingham. Who wouldn't love her delicious Albert Campion?"

Hector brought more plates, holding the kitchen door open for Sasha.

"Mother, you just like books with aristocrats as heroes." It was a conversation they'd had before.

"Yes, darling, I do. We get *such* a bad press. Like those footballers who help the homeless or demand free food for poor children. No one sees the *good* we do."

The connection between Marcus Rashford and the British aristocracy escaped everyone except Belinda, but Ginny looked happy. Hector glanced at Sasha, who was carrying an enormous bowl of salad. She winked at him, and seemed to be struggling not to laugh. Maybe things would be alright.

"*You* could be a titled sleuth, Hector," Belinda mused.

"I'd have to kill my brothers first. Given that there are two senior police officers at the table, it's probably best not to make any plans for that."

"I like a good detective story," said Sasha, "but I've never read Marjorie Allingham. Isn't she a bit old-fashioned?"

Belinda put her wine glass down and smiled. A genuine smile.

"Not at all. Good stories don't age," she said, "Try *Tiger in the Smoke*, *The Crime at Black Dudley* ... but my absolute favourite is *Look to the Lady*, because no one expects the villain to be a woman, even though it's staring them in the face from the start. And everyone thinks that they know what's going on, but they don't, so ... you need to read it, it's complicated and wonderful."

Sasha said she would.

After that the meal went well. Sasha admitted to having made the pavlova they had for dessert, and even Ginny mellowed after too many glasses of wine. Belinda had a single glass so she could drive them back to their hotel. She followed Sasha upstairs to check on Arwen, and they admired her sleeping form together.

"Talk to me for a minute, my dear," she said, so Sasha led her to Hector's room, and they sat next to each other on the bed.

"Did I pass?" Sasha asked, and Belinda grasped her hand.

"I could ask you the same thing," she said, "Speaking for myself, I would be delighted if you married Hector — and not only because I would see more of your lovely daughter. I see the way that Hector looks at you, and I would be a horrible sort of mother not to want him to be happy."

"You let his brother marry Ginny," said Sasha, and there was a moment of silence as it sank in. Then Belinda clapped a hand to her chest and roared with laughter.

"I know, I know ..." and they were both laughing, and it *was* going to be alright.

The three men heard the screams of laughter from upstairs and started smiling. Ginny frowned and asked where the bathroom was.

"Sasha?" Mal asked, when Ginny had gone.

"She's wonderful," said Hector dreamily, "I think I'm getting married."

Look to the Lady, Daniel thought. *It's been staring us in the face from the beginning.*

Chapter 22

The bottle of whisky was finished, and the woman had gone. He'd come to the end, and oh, he was so glad of it.

"It's Mel," said Daniel, when they were back in the car.

"What's Mel?"

"It's what Belinda said about that book she was going on about. *No one expects the villain to be a woman, even though it's staring them in the face from the start.* We've been looking at all the men — John Edwards, Mabon, Cai, Jack Wall — and we've missed the obvious."

"You're saying Mel killed the Edwards family?"

Daniel looked at Mal as if at an idiot.

"Don't be silly. John Edwards killed them. He was depressed, his wife was having an affair, and it pushed him over the edge. He was afraid of the press. He was being blackmailed and threatened, and he killed them and then he killed himself. You know it happens. You said so to Hart."

"You said ... oh never mind. So you think she killed Jack Wall then?"

"I'm pretty sure that was John Edwards too."

"Dan, you aren't making any sense."

"Mel was afraid, and it made her do stupid things. Veronica said as much when I asked her who would abandon a toddler, and she said people who are afraid do terrible things. I think Mel was afraid of being on her own. I think she thought she was going to lose Mabon, and she'd be a single parent again, with no money."

"So she did what?"

"I'm guessing here, but I think she threatened John Edwards with the press, because that's what he was terrified of. I think she was the one who suggested hiding Jack Wall's body and pretending he was still alive, and I think she was going to do the same with the Edwardses. I think she was using Harry to keep Mabon in order. She wanted financial security, and not to be on her own with her kids."

"And if you're right, what are we going to charge her with?"

"Perverting the course of justice? Illegal burial? Contempt of court? She's in the middle of it, making things happen, trying to manipulate everyone, and doing it so badly that people have died."

"She did steal Hayley's clothes. We can charge her with that."

"A psychologist would have a field day. Did she steal the clothes because she wanted to be Hayley? Have Hayley's life?"

"More likely she was going to sell them online."

"So why pretend that Harry was an Edwards?"

"Panic. We said we were the police, and even though we didn't look like coppers, she thought we'd come for Mabon. I was holding Harry. I think Harry had escaped and was going for a wander, because that's what toddlers do."

"Let me get this straight. The Edwards family was murder/suicide, Jack Wall's death was an accident, and everything else was incompetent blackmail?"

"Pretty much."

"Daniel Owen, I think you're drunk."

"I can be drunk and still be right."

"We've got to bring her in," Mal said, and Daniel nodded, "Maybe Cai will stump up for the solicitor again."

That was the problem, Daniel thought, right there in a nutshell. Cai was rich, or his family was, and Mel was poor. She'd tried to solve her problems with a man, and the temptation of making themselves *safe* in Gelli had been too much to resist. Tom and Bethany had felt the same temptation. Wanting the alternative life, that people like Cai and Mabon could have so easily, because of where they came from, or that Hayley could have because she'd married a rich footballer.

Jay Grieve had confirmed what Tom said about the cost of buying in to Holyoak Hall. "It costs a fortune to run, and there's a mortgage to pay. We bought the house for a song, but only because it was falling down, and we had to borrow to put it back together. Co-operative ownership is cheaper than buying yourself a little house in the suburbs, but it's not *free.*"

Jay had also told Daniel that Mabon and Cai had both invested in Holyoak, and sold their shares when they moved. Cai and Becca would be welcomed back, Mabon and Mel, not so much. "Only Cai fell under Michael's spell. He could be magnetic, you know."

"And Mel?"

"Mel wants someone else to look after her kids. She wants a man to look after her. She thought she'd found one. I could have told her what he was, but she wouldn't have listened. There are too many Mels bringing their problems to places like this. You think I'm hard? It's experience talking."

* * *

Mel said no. She wasn't going back to the police station. She was making sandwiches for a picnic, and that was what she was doing today, nothing else.

Cai said that he would get his solicitor, but Mel shook her head and carried on slicing cheese. Becca said, "We can all come with you Mel. We won't leave you on your own."

Daniel could hear thumps from upstairs suggesting Josh and Ben were using Josh's crutches in turn, which meant Josh's foot must be feeling better. Pixie was clinging to her mother's leg, and Mel was trying to shake her off. He glimpsed one of the other girls every few seconds out of the window, as she swung into view, and then disappeared. He heard a whine. *It's my turn. You said.*

"Ms Ward, Mel," Mal said, "if you don't come with us voluntarily, we will arrest you. Why don't you accept your friend's offer of a solicitor?"

"Mummiee," Pixie pulled at her mother's skirt.

"What? What? What?" Mel's voice rose higher and higher. Daniel saw the woman, the knife and the child, and heard the desperation in Mel's voice. Cai saw it too.

"Pixie, love, come and see what Becca's got for you," he said, but Pixie held on to her mother and ignored him.

"We only want to ask you a couple of things," said Mal in a voice as soft and gentle as melting chocolate. "We think you and Mabon were closest to John Edwards, that's all." It was the wrong thing to say.

"Not close enough," Mel snapped, "not close at all. I don't know why you're saying that. It isn't true. Mabon lied. We had nothing to do with them."

Daniel became aware that the noises from upstairs had stopped.

"We live here. That's all. Why would they have anything to do with us. They were rich. I didn't hear anything. I didn't see them."

Becca opened the front door and slipped out. A moment later the girls on the swing were quiet.

Cai walked towards the table, "Pixie, don't you want to see what Becca is doing with Betty and Amy?" He reached for the little girl's hand, but she pulled away. "I want to stay with Mummy."

"Mel, tell Pixie to go outside with the others, hey?"

"She can stay."

Now there was no doubting it. Pixie was a hostage, and everyone knew it but Pixie.

"It must be hard for you, without Mabon," Mal tried again, "You'd feel better if you talked about it, about John, and Hayley. I promise, you won't come to any harm, and Cai and Becca will look after the children."

Cai said that of course they would, in a voice that could seduce the birds from the trees.

"I've got nothing to talk about. I didn't see them. I didn't see John." Mel's hand was sweating as she held the knife. Daniel could see the slickness against the black plastic handle. He could feel her need to wipe her hand on her skirt, but she wasn't letting go of the knife. She wiped the other hand instead.

"Dafydd got out. That's why I was outside. Dafydd got out after I changed his nappy. I didn't see John."

The air in the room was solid with the efforts Daniel, Mal and Cai were making to stay calm. Even Pixie started to notice something wrong, and withdrew from her mother's side. Mel pulled her back, hard, and Pixie wailed.

They heard a new voice, high pitched and wobbly. Josh had materialised in the room, as silent as a ghost, despite his crutches.

"Mum, *I saw you*. You killed them. You killed Seren. *I saw you.*"

"I didn't kill anyone Josh. Stop lying. I was outside because of the baby."

"Mum, I saw you come out of Seren's house. Dafydd wasn't there. You killed them."

And then everything happened at once.

Mel screamed and lunged for Josh with the knife held high above her head. Cai went to grab Pixie, Daniel pulled Josh away from his mother and Mal pushed the kitchen table as hard as he could, hitting Mel in the thighs and slowing her down. Daniel snatched one of Josh's crutches and swung it at Mel, catching her knife hand and sending the knife clattering onto the floor. It was bloody and Daniel saw that Cai was bleeding. He and Mal tried to hold onto Mel, to push her onto the floor, but she fought and fought, slippery with sweat, biting and kicking, punching and scratching every time she got a hand free. Cai kicked the knife away under a cupboard, and ran to the front door.

He's running off?

But when the door opened it was to admit PC Jones, weighted down with his radio, baton, pepper spray and handcuffs, and it was all over.

* * *

The good news was that Cai wasn't injured, bar a scratch on his arm. The bad news was that the press were swarming over Gelli, PC Jones having left the barrier to help them with Mel.

Cai called his parents' firm, and they sent another, equally sharp, solicitor to represent Mel. He and Becca promised to take care of all the children, "Until things are sorted out." Daniel had to break it to them that they were both facing charges relating to Harry Bell's abduction, Jack Wall's body, and blackmail.

They left PC Jones with Becca and the children and took Cai, Josh and Mel to Melin Tywyll and the police station. Daniel insisted that their first aider look after Cai's arm before they spoke to him and then took him back to the same interview room he'd been in the day before.

"I don't want to get used to this," Cai said.

"Tell the truth then," Daniel replied, "I think we made it clear that we weren't letting this go. So far, you're looking at charges relating to Harry Bell's abduction, concealing Jack Wall's body, and blackmail."

"Blackmail?" Cai said, "Jack Wall's death was an accident. We were looking out for John. No one was going to believe he didn't mean to kill Jack. Not after he found him and Hayley together. Who was being blackmailed?"

If Cai hadn't spent so many days telling lies, Daniel might have believed him.

"You're an intelligent man Cai. You *know* you should have called 999 when Jack died. Our pathologist, who is bloody good, says that the chances of deliberately knocking Jack over so that he hit his head are infinitesimal. John might have hit him, but it wasn't murder. I don't know whose idea it was to hide the body, but you all knew about it. Someone was sending texts and emails. I don't know how you slept at night."

"John was paranoid about the press. Jack was famous. John was famous. It sounds bonkers now, but we were going to move the body away from here. Confuse everything. John was going to take Hayley and the girls away when it was found."

Daniel thought it sounded stupid enough to be true. And the hippies had shown themselves to be gold medalists at sowing confusion. It might even have worked. But he wasn't buying it.

"So you were all just looking after John Edwards," he asked drily, "You didn't want anything from him? It was a coincidence that he went to his solicitor to ask about giving Gelli Terrace to its tenants?"

"Fair exchange is no robbery."

"Cai, he's dead. He killed his wife and children. You don't think your *fair exchange* had something to do with that? His kids could see he was depressed, your kids could see it, you must have seen it. You did nothing. You let four people die because you wanted a house."

"He killed them because Hayley said she wanted a divorce. Nothing to do with the house. It was a crap marriage, but he was afraid that if she left, he'd take the girls. And the press thing. Like I say, he was paranoid."

Cai shrugged. His body language said that he really couldn't care less. Daniel didn't hit him, but it was close.

Veronica acted as an Appropriate Adult when they interviewed Josh. She recommended a local solicitor who was also present. Josh didn't have much to add to what he'd said earlier. He'd seen his mother come out of *Ty Gelli* in the very early morning, long before Daniel and Mel had run into Harry on the road. Mal explained that the girls and Hayley had died the night before, and that his mother couldn't have killed them. But had Josh heard a loud bang in the early morning?

"I think so. And there was lots of shouting."

Mal asked the next question very gently, not sure whether Josh would understand the implications.

"Did you hear the bang before your mother came out of the house?"

He understood.

"I'm not sure."

Mal asked whether Mel had been carrying anything when she came outside, and Josh said no. He was certain about that at least.

When Josh had gone, to wait with Cai, Daniel said, "She went back for Hayley's clothes, knowing they were all dead. They *cried* about those girls." There was nothing else to say.

Neither of them got anywhere with Mel. She consulted her solicitor and then *No Commented* like a veteran of the criminal justice system.

* * *

Superintendent Hart had been talking to the Crown Prosecution Service about what charges should be brought. She called Daniel and Mal into her office. For once she looked less than perfectly turned out. Her hair stuck up where she'd been running her hands through it, and there were half empty coffee cups on the desk.

"I don't know how to tell you this," she said, "but the CPS say none of it will stick. Too much hangs on the word of a confused ten year old. We can keep Mel Ward in overnight and see if she cracks in the morning, but that's the best I can offer."

"What about Harry Bell?" Daniel asked, "they all knew he'd been abducted."

"The abduction was down to Mabon, who's still in a coma. *We* know that the rest of them knew he'd been abducted, but we can't prove it. And you said yourself that the boys mother doesn't want to come back for a trial."

Daniel thought that she was right, and that the CPS were right too. He looked over at Mal, and saw the resignation in his face.

"We can't prove any of it." Daniel said, "All they have to do is say that John Edwards hid Jack Wall's body, or that Mabon told them he'd been given custody of Harry, and they could easily get the benefit of the doubt." Daniel had Tom and Bethany's story, but how would that hold up against all the others' denials? They could change their minds and go back to lying along with everyone else.

Hart said, "There doesn't seem much doubt that John Edwards did kill his family, though who knows why he waited so long to kill himself? Mel Ward could possibly tell us, but I don't think she will. John Edwards almost certainly killed Jack Wall, and I'm inclined to believe Hector Lord that it was an accident. Everything else? Sometimes police work stinks. Go home."

* * *

It wasn't the first time that they had poured time and resources into a case that resulted in no prosecutions, but this was worse because of the children.

"Harry Bell got a happy ending anyway," Mal said. Their chairs were out in the garden again, probably for the last evening in the current hot spell — rain was forecast for the next day.

"Except he won't see his dad. Monica won't be sorry, but maybe Harry will be."

"Who knows if Mabon is even going to wake up? And would you want little Harry in with that crowd?"

Daniel thought that Harry was better off in Italy with Monica. He wished her a good Italian man who would love her and Harry, and not tell lies. He suspected that it would take her a long time to trust anyone again.

Mal said, "Abby got a message from Jack Wall's parents. They're coming to formally identify him next week, and take him home to be buried. Abby can deal with them. She's talked to them so far."

"She helped me talk to the Edwardses too. What a bloody week."

"There's one good thing though. I remembered to call the number for the people who help ex-servicemen. They're coming to see James Protheroe. No one's going to make him to move, but he's going to be all on his own. I think he wants company."

"He wants a cleaner, that's for sure."

Mal grinned. "It was pretty awful."

"I've been in nicer crack dens."

"You've never been in a crack den."

"Have so."

Mal poked Daniel in the ribs. "Melin Tywyll is far too posh for crack dens."

Daniel poked him back.

There was the sound of a car coming up the track.

Mal stood up and peered. "It's the love birds. You know, the ones who like dead bodies."

Hector and Sasha got out of the car, leaving Arwen asleep in the back.

"We're only here for five minutes," Sasha said, "I wanted to tell you about the ginormous rock Hector wanted to buy me as an engagement ring."

"Only she wouldn't let me."

"I said you could fly round the world for less. First class."

"You'll be getting married then?" Daniel asked, "Please can I be a bridesmaid this time?"

"I'll think about it," said Sasha, "but I'll be honest, I don't think peach silk is right with your colouring, and you'd need to grow your hair a bit. To hold the fascinator."

"We just wanted to say thanks for last night. My mother has given us her blessing, and even Ginny managed to say congratulations. My father will fall into line."

"What about Arwen?"

Sasha smiled and Hector blushed brick red. "She was so sweet," he said, "asked if I would be Daddy Hector."

"I said only if we got a crack at the title," said Sasha, "but it seems that we *would* have to murder Hector's brothers. Anyway we have to go."

Mal picked up Sasha's left hand. An opal gleamed in a gold band on her ring finger. "I wanted something *pretty,*" she said, "not something expensive." And, in a most un-Sasha-like way, she turned away. "This getting married business is so *embarrassing.*"

"I'll let Mal be the bridesmaid," said Daniel, "Peach silk will look good on him."

When their visitors had gone, Daniel held Mal's hand.

"I'm going to see Megan in the morning," he said, "see if I can make things right again."

"You will."

Chapter 23

Dave was out in the garden with his nephew and niece, enjoying the weather while it lasted. Rain was forecast for the afternoon. Daniel and Megan sat in the kitchen looking into steaming mugs of coffee, neither of them knowing where to start. In the end, it was Megan.

"It's not healthy, always you and me against the world. I'm married. I have kids and a serious job."

Daniel said nothing.

"You have Mal, you don't need me to be the big sister all the time. And like I say, we have to learn to, well, grow up. Both of us."

Daniel couldn't see how his sister lying to him was an example of growing up. Somehow, he said so. Megan was the older of the twins, and those few minutes had given her the edge. She was the one in charge, the one who worried. He was the little boy who took her his problems. Later it had become mutual, only now she had decided, unilaterally, that it was over. No more shared secrets, and she called it growing up.

"OK, maybe I should have told you sooner." There was a silence, one that indicated that there was more. Megan smoothed her eyebrows, tucked her hair behind her ears.

"Dave said ..." she took a breath, "Dave said I should make my own decisions. That I had no confidence in myself unless I ran everything past you first. We had a row. The same row we've always had. About how I take my problems to you, not him. By the time I tell him anything, I've already decided what to do."

"You should have said." It didn't occur to him that was Dave's exact problem. Because he and Megan were *twins* and the rules were different.

"He thought it was funny at first. Me asking my brother if I should go out with him, then if I should marry him ..."

That wasn't how Daniel remembered it at all. Dave and Megan had used him as a go between. Seventeen year old Dave had wondered aloud whether Megan liked him, and seventeen year old Megan had asked if Dave was as nice as he seemed. As Dave was his best friend at school, he'd said yes to both. Perhaps there had been other boys who Megan had liked, and he'd said no, other boys who wondered if Megan liked them ... He took a drink of coffee. Megan might be wrong, but she was serious. This was where things changed and the old order ended.

"I told you I was pregnant, before I told Dave. He couldn't come to the scan appointment. I should have changed it, but I took you instead. So you knew we were having twins before he did. He's never been happy about it."

"You should have said." But he saw that she couldn't, not while he was deciding to buy the smallholding, or was desperate about promotion, or crying on her shoulder about Mal.

"He applied for the job in Spain, and he didn't tell me, because he didn't think he had a chance. He went for the interview in Manchester and they offered it to him on the spot. He wants it. It's a massive promotion, and he said he'd talk it over with his wife and get back to them the next day. And he was driving back from Manchester," Megan was pulling her hair, looking at the ends as if they had a message for her, "and he thought that he wouldn't be able to get back to them until I'd talked to you, and that you'd be in the middle of something ... and he thought that, well ..."

"You had to decide for yourself. Straight away."

"Yep."

"And you wanted him to take the job, and that's what you'd have said to me anyway, but he didn't know that." Because he did know her better than anyone. She wouldn't have asked him, she'd have told him, and expected his support, and he'd have given it. She'd stopped pulling at her hair, and there were tears in her eyes. He reached for his coffee, then changed his mind and reached for her hand instead.

"It's fine," he said, "Go to Spain, and have nice weather, and good food, and a house with a pool, and see if I care." His throat had closed, and he felt the heat of imminent tears behind his cheeks, but he meant what he was saying. This *was* growing up. He didn't like it much, but he suspected that it was probably a good idea. He held onto that thought and the tears faded back into something he could swallow.

"It's a habit," he said, "You would have made your own decision, but we've got into the habit of pretending to consult each other. Habits are hard to break. That's all. I'm still going to tell you everything though. Everything. In detail."

"No way! Why do you think I want to go to Spain?" She was smiling and so was he.

"There's this thing Mal wants to do in bed, and I'm not sure ..." she hit him, as the door burst open. His nephew threw himself at Daniel, talking about snails — *snails?* — and his niece grabbed his arm, the coffee cup-holding arm, and then they were all mopping up coffee, and Daniel was asking about the job in Spain, and not understanding the answer, because Dave did something in software engineering, whatever that was, and then Megan was asking him and Mal to come round for dinner, and then it was time to go home.

* * *

He was getting much too fond of driving the Audi. He loved the way that it didn't lean round corners, he loved the automatic gearbox, the electric windows, the comfortable seats. Then he turned up the steep track to his house, and remembered why he'd bought a Land Rover. Even at snail speed (what was it about snails today?), the Audi hated the potholes, and the mud, and the way the track turned into a stream after rain, and in the winter, they mostly just left it on the road. But in this weather, and on good roads, the Audi was great. He parked next to the Land Rover, to the side of the house, not in front, because who wanted to look at a car, when they had a view over the valley, to the hills beyond?

It took him a second to realise that there shouldn't have been a Land Rover there at all. His Land Rover had gone for scrap. He was programmed to expect to see it parked next to the house, where it had been for years, so to see it there felt normal. Only it couldn't be. Except it was. *His* Land Rover. The mobile skip. He recognised the number plate, and he recognised the worn steering wheel and the cup holder he'd stuck on to the dashboard. It was definitely *his* Land Rover.

It had been re-sprayed a shiny dark grey. The tyres were all new. There were no dents in the panels or the doors. The snorkel was new. The seats were new. The windows must be new because most of them had been broken. It was cleaner than he had ever seen it.

Daniel didn't hear Mal come up behind him because he was too busy examining his old friend to notice. He felt the arms round his waist and warm breath in his ear.

"Like it?"

He turned to face Mal. "Did you do this? For me?"

"Did I do the right thing?"

"It's beautiful."

"It's better than I expected, almost respectable."

Daniel hugged Mal as hard as he could. "Thank you so much. I don't know what else to say. Just thank you."

"I was terrified that you'd actually *like* one of the other cars I made you look at, or that you'd start going to see second hand Defenders on your own." Mal felt in his pocket and gave Daniel a set of keys attached to a big 'D' in rainbow colours.

"It must have cost a fortune."

"Only a small one. Like you always say, they're indestructible. It's got a reconditioned engine and gear box, but pretty much everything else is just mended. The new seats were for me. I got fed up with the springs sticking into my arse."

"Wimp. Want to come for a drive?"

Mal smirked. "By an amazing coincidence, I have a picnic and a flask of coffee in the kitchen."

Compared to the Audi, the Land Rover felt like being in a donkey cart, not that Daniel had ever driven a donkey cart, but he could imagine. It was noisy and the gear changes were still the equivalent of shouting instructions to a donkey. But the car took the potholes in its stride, and so what if it leaned a bit round the corners, he could see over the hedges again. And Land Rovers didn't fall over. He'd proved that by driving it off the road and down into a river. For the first time ever he worried about his lovely new paintwork. But he couldn't stop smiling.

"I can't believe you did this. For me."

"I can't believe you didn't find out. You missed your mobile skip. It was a no brainer."

Daniel smiled until his cheeks ached.

They met an even shinier, newer, 4x4 coming the other way on the narrow lane, driven by a middle aged woman. She gave Daniel a look mixed with panic and entitlement. In return Daniel gave her a thumbs up, put the Land Rover into one of its many reverse gears and whizzed up an unnecessarily steep and rocky farm track, sides scratching against the brambles. He grinned.

"She was right next to a lay by," Mal growled.

"Don't be mean. You saw her face. She's frightened to reverse."

"You shouldn't buy something you can't reverse," Mal grumbled, "And you've scratched the paintwork." But he was laughing.

"It's like spilling wine on a new sofa. It's going to happen, so you may as well get it over with."

They trundled on, until Daniel turned up another impossibly steep and rocky lane, marked, of course with a sign suggesting that only a fool would keep going. It was in Welsh, but Mal understood *Pergyl* and *Arafwch.* He didn't comment.

"Stop pretending you can't read that sign."

"I don't need to read it. It's like one of those signs that says *Drive Safely.* As if you got up one day and decided: *today I'm going to drive as dangerously as possible."*

"Either you tell me what that sign said, or there's no sex for a week."

"There's likely."

"You *know* what it said. I know you know. I speak to you in Welsh when you're half asleep sometimes, *and you answer.* You're not fooling me any more Maldwyn Kent."

Mal crossed his arms and stared out of the window, face creased into an exaggerated frown. The lane got steeper and Daniel shifted into an even lower gear. The Land Rover kept moving.

Mal mumbled something under his breath about following instructions.

"What was that?"

"I said, it's dangerous, drive slowly. As instructed by the fucking signpost. *Cariad."*

Daniel looked at his outrageously handsome boyfriend and laughed. "I think that's the first Welsh word you've ever said to me."

"That's only because swear words are the same in both languages."

The road ended at a tiny turn around, not big enough to be called a car park. A single rickety picnic table stood on a patch of rough grass. Clouds were beginning to cross the sky, each bringing a moment of cool shade.

"Come and see."

Daniel led Mal over to the table, and there it was, Wales, spread out at their feet. The river valley far below, and beyond the river, the bare Clwydian hills with their Iron Age forts, and beyond them, the mountains of Snowdonia, far away, rocky summits clear and sharp against the sky, colours changing as the clouds passed overhead.

There was nothing to say, they leaned back against the table, arms around each other, and drank it in.

"Picnic." Mal said after a while. They sat so that they could see the view and ate their sandwiches and drank their coffee, and Daniel thought that it really didn't get any better than this.

"Tell me about London, and this job," he said in the end, because he wanted to know.

"Only if you tell me what's been bothering you."

"You first."

Mal told him; about his father, the violence, being forced to leave, cut off from everyone and everything he knew.

"It was summer, and there was an end in sight. I got a cash-in-hand job washing up, and a place to crash in a squat. I only had to do it for a month and then I started at Hendon, with food and showers and a proper bed. For kids like Ethan, it's forever."

Daniel leaned against him and stared out at the hills.

"You have to go," he said, "you hate it here, and it's something you need to do. It needs doing and there's no one better qualified. If you don't do it now, while it's the latest idea, the powers-that-be will go on to the next thing and it'll be forgotten, another initiative that never made it out of the strategy papers."

"Will you come with me?"

Daniel turned and buried his face in Mal's shoulder, smelling his cologne and his skin, warm and clean. Mal's arm tightened around him.

"I don't know if I can," he said, I don't even know if I want to be a policeman any more. I'm a mess."

"You're the best policeman I know."

"I let Andy Carter die. I let you get shot. It's all too much."

"Tell me," Mal said.

"I can't."

They sat in silence, Mal watching the clouds, and Daniel pressing himself into Mal's body.

"I won't go," Mal said, "I'm not leaving you like this."

Daniel sat up, and pulled Mal's face to look at him.

"I want you to go. I'll miss you like hell, but it's only bloody London, not the moon. I'm not giving you up, not again, but you have to go and do this job."

"You do know I love you?"

"Maldwyn, you repaired my Land Rover. You hate it here and you've stayed. You've been practicing Welsh in secret with Sophie. You iron linen shirts for me. Yes, I know you love me. And I love you."

Daniel hoped that it would be enough.

* * *

Read on, for the opening chapter of **Too Many Fires**, *the next book in the series...*

214

* * *

*The opening of **Too Many Fires**, Book Five of the Daniel Owen Welsh Mysteries..*

* * *

Daniel Owen put the tomatoes out in the sun, so that they would be warm and juicy in time for lunch. A lunch he was planning to make entirely from his own produce. His fingers were stained and pungent from picking the tomatoes, and his feet were grey with dust, but he felt the heat on his skin and he was a man at peace. If he could somehow make a living this way he thought, then he would hand in his warrant card with joy, and think only of trees. He would plant walnuts and build an orangery. He would let his hair grow and the soil accumulate in the creases of his hands. He would get chickens. His few woody acres would collect more carbon than any of his neighbours' bald fields, planted only with sheep and thistles, and they would stop calling him a hobby farmer, he would find a way to tell Mal he was sorry and please could they try again, he would pay off the mortgage, sleep without nightmares, and

215

then the phone rang.

"I'll be there as soon as I can," he said, and then he called his sister and said sorry, lunch was off, again. He wanted to be sick. Or smash something. Instead he got into the car and followed the directions his sergeant had provided.

* * *

As he drove, he wondered how long the council would be able to carry on repairing the road. Every winter another section of hillside slid away, and another few bits of carriageway collapsed into the river below. Better to think about the state of the roads than to acknowledge the dread threatening to constrict his breathing and close his throat. He was not having a breakdown, he was over Mal, he was just sorry to be losing his day off *and that was all.* He knew his colleagues thought he'd withdrawn into misery, but it was either that or give in his notice.

The directions sent him up a narrow lane with trees crowding in on both sides, and glimpses of half hidden log cabins. The entrance to the holiday park appeared without warning. He turned in and saw more cabins and several police cars.

A uniformed officer was waiting by the gate to point him into an empty field and to write his name into the official record. The white crime scene tent was stark against the sky, nicely balanced by the black mortuary van.

"Scenes of Crimes says it's OK to walk anywhere sir, they've checked this area. The pathologist is waiting for you in the tent; they want to move the body."

Daniel didn't want to look inside the tent but that's what paid the bills.

The victim was lying on his stomach, head away from them. Daniel counted three bullet holes in the man's back, and above the neck, a bloody mess of bone and brain. Bile rose in his throat and he turned to the pathologist, his friend Hector Lord.

"Not nice," said Hector.

Daniel focussed hard on what had been a solidly built, middle aged man with a dark tan and smooth skin. He was dressed in good quality clothes and expensive soft leather loafers.

Right arm underneath him, the left thrown out to the side as if to save himself from falling. The visible arm was tattooed with what looked like part of an illuminated manuscript. He thought it might be a letter J twirled about with leaves, but it was half hidden in the shadows.

"What can you tell me?" Daniel asked.

"Best guess is that he was killed right here - there's nothing to indicate that the body was moved. I'd say he's been dead at least twelve hours, but not more than twenty four. Again best guess, sometime yesterday late evening. If it's OK with you, I'd like to get him shifted ASAP because it's getting hot already."

Daniel nodded, and the mortuary attendants trundled their trolley up the field.

Outside the tent, Bethan was waiting for him, looking cool and professional. Her hands twitched with the urge to reach up and comb his hair and check his fingernails for dirt. His first reaction was anger. Then guilt. His sergeant couldn't help behaving like a Mam any more than he could help resenting it.

She spoke: "Morning, Boss. Provisional ID on the body is a Derek Smith - driving license and credit cards in his pocket. If it is Smith, then he's one of the owners of the Holiday Park. Found by a Jonathan Cole, out walking his dog."

Bethan had already organised the Scenes of Crime team, and uniformed officers to keep the public from indulging their curiosity. House to house - or cabin to cabin - enquiries had started. The Park's manager had been located and was waiting with DC Rees. He asked what she knew about the Park. In answer she showed him a website on her phone as they walked.

Maes y Coed Holiday Park. A hundred Scandinavian style Holiday Lodges in a beautiful woodland setting. Own a Holiday Lodge, or just come and visit! Heated Swimming Pool, Play Areas, Games Room, Bar and Clubhouse.

Dark brown cabins had been dropped at random onto a wooded hillside, stilts levelling them against the slope, ferns taking advantage of the dampness underneath. The path away from the field led into dark shade, cabins tucked under the spreading branches of conifers and fully grown oaks, roofs covered in layers of thick green moss and leaf mould. Then, they came out into the sun again, and the trees were further apart; tall ashes looking spindly and frail amongst the oaks and beeches. Ruthlessly clipped cypresses provided privacy for some cabins while others nestled amongst straggly hollies and alders. Ivy and bramble crept out from the hedges and leaves poked through every crack in the tarmac.

A few cabins sat neatly framed with gravel and well-groomed plants in matching pots. A couple more had building materials stacked outside, ready for a bit of weekend DIY. One seemed to be occupied by twentysomethings just back from a festival; Leonard Cohen playing quietly, Indian print floor cushions to sit on, rainbow bunting framing the deck.

But other cabins appeared almost derelict, holes in the decking, rotten window frames and no signs of recent care.

"This isn't like any other holiday park I've been to," said Bethan, "It's like there aren't any rules. The places we used to take the boys had rules for everything. Where you could park, how many chairs on the deck, everything smart, identical and in its proper place."

"I bet even this place has rules against shooting the owner." Daniel said.

The manager of the Park didn't look like an enforcer of rules. A small, unhappy looking woman, she paced the small distance from one end of the shop to the other. She looked to be in her forties, and as if she'd had a hard life, face starting to wrinkle from too many cigarettes, her hair dyed an unlikely shade of strawberry blond.

"Mrs Kelly Howard? I'm Detective Chief Inspector Owen and this is my colleague Detective Constable Rees. We have some questions for you about the park."

Kelly opened her mouth then wrapped her arms around herself, as if to hold herself together and nodded.

"Tell me what's going on," she said. It wasn't a request.

Reception was a desk and a couple of chairs at one end of the small shop, next to a door marked Private. The rest of the space was filled with leaflet and guide book racks, an ice cream cabinet, a fridge with milk, cheese, bacon and pasta sauce, and shelves with playing cards, beach balls, chocolate and crisps.

"This morning the body of a man was discovered on your field," Daniel said and got a tight nod in return. "I'm sorry to have to tell you that it appears to be one of the owners of the park, Mr Derek Smith. We are treating the death as suspicious. I need to know about Mr Smith's role here, when he was last seen, and I need a list of everyone who was here yesterday and last night."

Daniel could get no sense of whether Kelly Howard was shocked or surprised by his statement. But she nodded as if she understood what he'd said and then went on the offensive.

"This is our busiest weekend. I need to open the bar and the pool. I'm on my own. I've got people checking in and out and cabins that need cleaning.I need you to go so that I can get on."

Daniel was sure that he heard Charlie's mouth fall open. He wondered at the absence of even a token word of sorrow at the loss of a man's life, a man she presumably dealt with regularly.

"I don't think you'll be opening today, Mrs Howard. Were you expecting to see Mr Smith?"

"I don't have time for this now."

"The sooner you answer our questions, the sooner we'll be gone. Were you expecting Mr Smith?" There was no way anything was re-opening until it had been searched, but for now he needed some basic information. The argument could wait.

"I never know when they're coming. Either they say they'll be here and don't show up, or they arrive at a moment's notice. So no, I wasn't expecting him. He might not have been coming to see me at all. You can ring them and explain why everything is closed and there are policemen everywhere."

It wasn't the first time a witness had assumed police omniscience and delivered information making no sense at all. Patiently Daniel teased out the essentials: Derek Smith and his brother-in-law were joint owners of the Park, but visited rarely. Apart from Kelly and some casual cleaners, the only other staff member was a groundsman/handyman called Pete. Most of the cabins on the Park were privately owned, others owned by the Park itself. He didn't ask why so many cabins were falling down. A list of who owned what was grudgingly provided. By the time he had the list in his hands he needed either a nap or a strong drink.

Kelly Howard continued asking when she could open the shop and the pool, as if business as usual could continue around the murder of her boss. He didn't know whether she was being deliberately obtuse, or if she genuinely didn't understand.

Daniel looked over at Charlie "Let us get you a glass of water, Mrs

Howard. You've had a shock."

Charlie disappeared into the bar and came back with a half pint glass filled with water. Kelly put her hand around the glass but didn't drink.

"I don't want you here. I'm sorry about Derek, but I've got a park to run. People want food, and drinks, and to use the pool."

Daniel wondered how to get through to her.

"Mrs Howard? Kelly? The park is a crime scene. Everything here will stay closed until we have completed our search."

Kelly stood up with a jerk, knocking the glass over on the desk, splashing water over herself and him. "No," she said, "no, no, no. Come back tomorrow. It won't be so busy. I'll have Pete to help. We can't have you here today." She was starting to sob with frustration, jabbing a tissue at the water on her clothes.

"Mrs Howard, there isn't a choice here. A man is dead. We are searching the park and we are doing it today. Everything will remain closed. Now please try to calm down."

Instead she picked up the glass and threw it at the wall, sending glass fragments flying, then turned away and stood sobbing, her shoulders hunched and her hands covering her face. Daniel felt a sting as a piece of glass hit his cheek. When he pulled it off, his fingers were bloody.

Charlie raised his eyebrows in a question.

"Let her be," said Daniel quietly.

"Your cheek is bleeding, sir, quite a lot."

Daniel peered at the cut on his cheek in the toilet mirror, ran his shirt under the tap and used it to clean up his face and neck. There was a lot of blood for a little cut. He leaned his forehead onto the cool mirror and closed his eyes. He wanted to go home to the peace and almost competence he had felt before the phone rang. Instead he pulled on his emergency shirt and his work face and went back out into the sun.

Bethan is right thought Daniel, there aren't any rules here.

* * *

It was the glasses that Daniel saw first. Big round dark frames for an awkward man to hide behind, except that this man wasn't awkward. Behind the glasses, green eyes, looking out curiously. Daniel took in the dark hair, still damp from the shower, the long wiry limbs, bare feet with painted nails, but mostly the curious eyes looking into his, smiling at him, recognising him. The effect was shocking.

"Mr Jonathan Cole?" Daniel had forgotten Jonathan's surname, though his memories of the man himself had come flooding back the minute he opened the door.

"Yes. The man who found the body. Not a role I was looking for. Come in and take a seat. Can I make you a drink?"

Daniel would have refused, but Bethan was quicker "Tea would be lovely - no milk for either of us, thanks."

While Jonathan filled the kettle, and arranged teapot and mugs on a tray, Daniel looked round. The inside of the cabin was open, and painted white. There were bookshelves everywhere, all overfull. Books and papers were piled on the floor like fallen leaves. It was cool in here, under the trees and out of the sun.

When he'd poured, Jonathan sat down, pushed his glasses up his nose, and looked expectantly at Daniel and Bethan. "So," he said.

"We understand that early this morning you found a body, that we are provisionally identifying as Derek Smith, in the field behind your cabin," said Daniel, taking refuge from his confusion in formality, "Can you tell us why you were there?"

"I was walking Flora, early because it's hot, before I start work." The dog looked up at Jonathan, hearing her name. A small dog, some kind of whippet cross, with delicate features. She tucked her nose back under her paws.

"What do you do for work, Mr Cole?"

"Editing books mostly."

"Did you touch the body?"

"No. I knew that he was dead before I saw ...". Daniel saw Jonathan pale and swallow hard. He felt the nausea rise in his own throat in sympathy.

Jonathan's face tightened and he breathed slowly and deliberately. In his mind's eye, Daniel saw Derek Smith's body as Jonathan had seen it, felt the early morning grass under his feet as Jonathan must have felt it, and shared the fear that the image of that shattered head would never go away.

You poor bugger, welcome to my shitty world.

"I'm sorry, but we need to ask these questions," Daniel heard Bethan sigh. "Did you hear or see anything unusual last night or this morning? Loud noises last night, lights, anything you weren't expecting."

"There were fireworks at some point, and a bit of noise from the bar ... but, no, nothing unusual, sorry. What happened to Derek?"

Daniel didn't answer. Instead he asked another question. "Did you get on well with Mr Smith?"

"Sure, he can be fun ... makes lots of jokes at his own expense ... he's always got a story about his son, or somewhere he's been ... he's OK really."

"But not everyone liked him?"

Jonathan answered without pausing, "Lots of the cabin owners hate him. Him and his partner. People say they're criminals. It's what people here talk about mostly. But they live and let live, and that's what matters to me."

"You live here all the time?" Bethan asked.

"That would be against planning regulations. We're all supposed to leave for a month on the first of January, but no one comes round to check if we've gone." He smiled at Daniel. Bethan saw and scowled.

Jonathan fell silent and looked out of the cabin windows. Daniel followed his gaze up to the trees, still in full leaf with the intense green of late summer. Triangular windows filled the apex of the roof, giving more views of trees, some leaves just planes of vivid yellow, bright against the shade around them. Daniel watched as a squirrel ran up a tree trunk and onto thinner and thinner branches, until the last one was no thicker than string, before it leapt to the next tree. From the corner of his eye he saw that Jonathan was watching the same squirrel and he smiled.

He went to put his empty mug down, and missed the table. They watched it fall, and roll harmlessly until it settled next to a pile of paper.

That's me, falling. Again.

"Where were you last night Mr Cole?" Bethan's voice broke in.

"I was here."

"Did you see anyone? Talk to anyone?"

"I walked Flora round the Park. I think I said hello to a few people. No real alibi if that's what you're asking."

Daniel said "We have to check," and Jonathan nodded and reached absently for a cotton bandana, and polished his glasses. Daniel felt Jonathan's quietness filling the space, and he wanted to sit there with him, watching the trees and allowing the time to pass.

"That Cole is odd," said Bethan, "and he spoke as if you knew each other."

"Shock," said Daniel, not wanting to think about just how disconcerting he'd found Jonathan, or how strange it was to find him here, among the trees.

The cabins on either side of Jonathan's were a study in contrasts. On the right, a couple sat under a smart umbrella, with matching furniture, on a freshly painted deck extending almost all the way round the cabin. Hanging baskets hung from the eaves. The windows had been replaced, with blinds added to keep the sun at bay. The table held a bottle and glasses, paperback books, and a newspaper.

On the other side, a cabin was tucked into the hedges, like Jonathan's. But unlike Jonathan's there was little sign of life. The parking place was overgrown with moss, bushes beginning to colonise the space in front of the door. There was no deck, only a couple of very green looking plastic chairs and a rotting table. From where they stood Daniel couldn't tell if the cabin was inhabited, or even habitable. Daniel thought that it was being reabsorbed back into the wood.

He asked who else Bethan and her team had spoken to.

"Most people have gone out for the day or else they're on their decks sipping cold Prosecco, and reading romantic novels. At eleven in the morning. Like them." She nodded towards the cabin to their right. "Nothing useful, so far. For the summer holidays it's bloody quiet."

Daniel produced the list of cabin numbers and names from Kelly Howard. "Lots of these are shown as belonging to the Park, but no one's using them. This place should be buzzing."

Bethan shrugged. "No rules" she said.

About the Author

I hope that you've enjoyed this book as much as I enjoyed writing it. In another life, I spent time researching intentional communities, so it was good to put some of that knowledge to use. It's worth saying that the intentional communities in this book, and their residents, are completely fictional.

This is a more 'domestic' book than the earlier ones, crime without criminals if you like. I wanted to show how ordinary people do terrible things, without setting out to cause harm. The next book is *not* like that. If you want to get a flavour, the opening section is included as chapter 24...

I'd be very grateful if you felt like leaving a review on Amazon for other readers.

A link to my website is below. There some extra Daniel Owen stories on the site, plus a sign up to my newsletter — first to get the news! I also have a Facebook page: Ripley Hayes Author.

Acknowledgements

Thanks are due to: Sharon Cox, Denise Hayes, Austin Gwin, Bill Millward, the Octopeople, Jo Rabbani, and Lou Sugg - and everyone else who has taken the time to be encouraging, on the interwebs and IRL.

Cover Design from Pixel Studios

You can connect with me on:

🌐 https://www.ripleyhayes.com

◼ https://www.facebook.com/Ripley-Hayes-Author-107043001322058

Subscribe to my newsletter:

✉ https://www.ripleyhayes.com

Also by Ripley Hayes

Ripley Hayes is the author of the DI Daniel Owen Welsh Mysteries series:

Undermined

Dark Water

Leavings

A Man

Too Many Fires (pre-order on Amazon)

A new series featuring Daniel and Private Investigator Teema Crow will begin in autumn 2021.

Manufactured by Amazon.ca
Bolton, ON

25834279R00136